THESE MEMORIES
DO NOT BELONG TO US

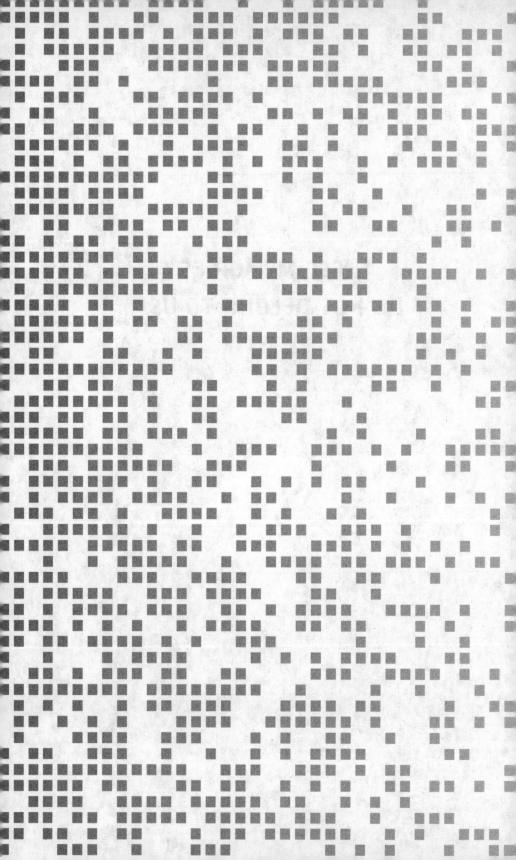

THESE
MEMORIES
DO NOT
BELONG TO US

A CONSTELLATION NOVEL

YIMING MA

MARINER BOOKS

New York   Boston

THESE MEMORIES DO NOT BELONG TO US. Copyright © 2025 by Yiming Ma. All rights reserved. Printed in the United States of America. No part of this book may be used or reproduced in any manner whatsoever without written permission except in the case of brief quotations embodied in critical articles and reviews. For information, address HarperCollins Publishers, 195 Broadway, New York, NY 10007.

HarperCollins books may be purchased for educational, business, or sales promotional use. For information, please email the Special Markets Department at SPsales@harpercollins.com.

The Mariner flag design is a registered trademark of HarperCollins Publishers LLC.

FIRST EDITION

Designed by Jennifer Chung
Background noise texture © Guss No/stock.adobe.com
Mosaic pattern © Flow 37/stock.adobe.com

Library of Congress Cataloging-in-Publication Data
has been applied for.

ISBN 978-0-06-341348-1

25 26 27 28 29 LBC 5 4 3 2 1

For survivors and the stories that saved me

MESSAGE FROM OWNER

███████ at ██ : ███████

When I was a boy, my mother used to tell me stories of a world before memories could be shared between strangers. Although all the stories took place long before she had been born, it was easy to believe that she had witnessed them firsthand. Her lips would tremble, her voice rising with excitement. Wistfully, she would describe a time when our ancestors shared their thoughts using nothing more than words, such a primitive tool to allow others to experience their most vivid, personal memories.

Some of the Memory Epics from which she drew her stories must have been censored already by the Party. Any loyal patriot would have deleted these memories—for instance, the tale of an armless swimmer during the Cultural Revolution, when citizens still raised children with disabilities. Or the meta-creational Epic revolving around the Incineration of Ri-Ben, a military campaign that our youth no longer study. Why keep any of them, if they might put us at risk of the Party's wrath? Had one of our neighbors reported us, our family's entire collection of memories might have been confiscated, and not only the ones we should have known to hide.

Since I was a child, I accepted that my mother was not an ordinary woman, not least because of her choice to raise me alone. Late in life, she decided that she wanted to be a mother, and she had refused to allow the absence of a suitable partner, or the downgrading of her social credit score, to stop her. I've always thought that one Qin proverb epitomized her fearlessness: even if the sky collapsed, she would use it as a blanket to warm her body. So why would the memories stored in such a woman's Mindbank be any less remark-able? Since the devices are directly installed into the hippocampi in our brains, I like to think of her Mindbank as simply the extension of her mind. Still, my mother was careful never to send any sensitive memories to my Mindbank, to avoid unwanted attention.

Now that I reflect on that precious time together, perhaps that was why she told me all those stories via voice in the privacy of our bedrooms, back when we were permitted to stop our Mindbanks from logging data at home, and away from any neighbors who lived in our Tower.

All my life, my mother had tried to protect me. So why would she risk everything by leaving me such a dangerous inheritance?

IT IS HARD TO IMAGINE A WORLD WHEN MINDBANKS DID NOT exist. After all, none of the prosperity we enjoy in Qin would be pos-sible without their invention. Before Mindbanks, every military sci-entist conducted their research in solitude. The only way they could collaborate was via voice or trading words across physical screens; think of all the meaning and nuance lost in every exchange! When the first Mindbank prototypes were tested by the military, our rate of scientific innovation began to accelerate exponentially. Without them, it is doubtful whether Qin would have been able to defend it-self against the Western powers that oppressed our ancestors, much less crush our enemies once and for all in the War.

Mindbanks made Qin into this great empire. So it is natural that for most of my life, I could not comprehend my mother's distaste toward Memory Capitalism: the buying and selling of Memory Epics that rep-resents the bedrock of our economy.

Once, when my mother casually asked what memories had been recently assigned for my education, and I proudly recited a patriotic passage as my answer—she laughed so loudly that I worried she was unwell. To my surprise, she stood and squeezed my shoulder, whispering in my ear words that sounded as if they'd come from some forgotten historian: that the Party's greatest triumph lay not in any scientific breakthroughs but rather its understanding that we all share a deep longing for social harmony, even at the cost of remembering our true histories.

What did she mean? This happened only a few days before the Gaokao exam, which would determine my future. I can still recall my confused silence, not quite comprehending but reluctant to ask her to clarify for fear of prolonging our memories of the conversation. It was around this period that the Party mandated that every Qin citizen keep their Mindbank streaming at all times, reassuring us that the data would be used only to improve the quality of entertainment, rather than for surveillance. Naturally, the Party believed in protecting the privacy of its citizens.

Another time in my youth, I asked if my mother might allow me to explore her Mindbank, and to my surprise, she refused.

What if I told you that some of my most-accessed memories belong in the Criminal Archives? my mother said. *Would you still want to see them?*

I drew back, stung. Walking away, I assumed that her response had been sarcastic because she wanted her son to work hard to build his own wealth of memories. It wasn't until ten moons ago that I revisited that conversation—on the day my mother breathed her last, and her Mindbank transferred to me her entire collection of Memory Epics. Including those that had inspired the bedtime stories from my childhood.

For a long time, I did not dare open my inheritance. Irrespective of the fact that the memories had been sent automatically, the Qin estate laws had recently been revised so that all passed-down assets would be stored and eventually reviewed by the Censors. Once processed, if any part of the inheritance became flagged by the Party, who knew what punishment would descend upon me? But when I ultimately entered the memories, compelled by the grief of losing my mother and the guilt of avoiding her final gift, I was stunned by what I found.

Certain memories were so corrupted during the transfer that my Mindbank restarted upon trying to access them. But the stories she did successfully send reflect the very journey of how Qin became the glorious empire where I and my fellow citizens live. And despite their illicit nature, and my shock that my mother would possess such a collection, I could not resist.

I proceeded to experience every single memory.

The Party may not want us to remember our past. But this history is too important to keep hidden within my family. Given the imminent advancements in Mindbank technology, I would not be surprised if the rumors are true and the Party will soon be able to search across all devices and delete any seditious memories, even if they were never uploaded onto any public Cloud. It is a matter of time before my inheritance undergoes its scheduled review by the Censors; surely then, the Red Guards will arrest me and confiscate my mother's stories once and for all.

What will be left of her then? Will I even be able to remember her? Growing up, I never met my biological father, so my mother was all I had. I rarely misbehaved, wanting to be a good child to make her proud. Perhaps I still harbor such desires, even after her death. I never want to forget the warmth of her voice, the tenderness with which she used to sing me to sleep whenever her stories excited me too much to rest.

No, I cannot bear living without her memories. So before that day arrives, I invite you to experience her stories. Even if the cost of sharing these truths is my freedom.

FORGIVE ME. I CANNOT REVEAL MORE DETAILS, AT LEAST NOT until you've entered these memories and assumed the same risks I have. My decision to release these Memory Epics on this unencrypted Cloud, for every Mindbank to access, stems from my belief that it might have been my mother's wish as well. She taught me that certain stories were too valuable to hoard as wealth, the way powerful families did to preserve their assets and influence across generations; rather, we have a collective duty to share them freely for the good of our society.

Should you decide to enter, do not be afraid to engage with these stories in any order. Embrace your freedom: there is no need to reproduce the precise cadence in which she told them. Some Memory Epics, created before the War using obsolete technology, may appear more fantastical than the ones that came later, especially those adapted from spoken or written histories. Still, I marvel at the infinite permutations of Memory Epics, as each story transforms and optimizes itself for every unique Mindbank. My hope is that the memories faithfully represent the stories of ordinary people—before, during, and after our society was irrevocably transformed—as we each sought our own ways to survive.

The last memory was drawn from my mother's own life, the only tale in this collection that she never shared with me via voice. Although I gently ask you to leave her story for the end, I know I have no right to dictate your path forward.

None of these memories belong to me anyway. Not anymore, and never again.

MAP OF MEMORIES

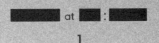

PATIENCE AND VIRTUE
AND CHESS AND AMERICA

Before the Qin-American orphanage opened its doors, the building had been a private school for children in what used to be Washington, DC. When the cherry blossoms bloomed every spring, the school's phones would begin ringing off the hook, overwhelmed by the wealthy, mostly American-white parents calling in favors to get their children admitted. It did not matter to these parents that the neighborhood where the school was located was not fully gentrified, that gangs pushed pills a few streets away, for as long as ex–Navy SEAL guards were still hired to inspect every car passing through its gates, what cause did they have to worry?

Hao was eight years old when he first stared at the brick behemoth of a building that swallowed up the entire block. Late for a meeting, his father had asked their driver to drop him off in front of the school's dark gates, oblivious to the security procedures for new students. By the time Hao managed to get seated in history class, the first lecture on the French Revolution had already ended.

He was seventeen now. Although he had already earned his Qin driver's license, not long after the country had renamed itself to honor China's first emperor, his father still demanded their driver escort him everywhere. Hao had argued that the streets were largely devoid of American-whites now, especially adults, but his father had silenced him with a look. In that withering glare, Hao saw the entirety of his father's derision:

What do you know? You have not been there for three years.

It was true. His father had flown them back to Qin a month before the War started. When Hao left, the city was still Washington, DC, and the country was called America without anything before its name. Land of the free, home of the brave. At least the new Qin colony had been permitted to keep most of its flag with the stripes, although the fifty white stars had been replaced with five yellow ones.

As his driver pulled into the parking lot, the boy realized that the school's tall and once-intimidating gates had been removed. What happened to the SEALs? Had they been replaced with AI security? On their drive, Hao had been astonished to see rampant weeds sprouting from the cracked roads, next to blocks of homes with boarded-up windows, paint peeling from their walls. He shook his head, reminding himself that there was little reason to make such investments in security anymore; the building was no longer an overpriced liberal arts haven.

Who would stoop to stealing from orphans, especially American white ones?

The car fell silent as the driver turned off its antiquated diesel engine using a steel key. Hao messaged him to stay behind in the car via his new Mindbank, recently installed in his right temple. Pushing open the bulletproof door, he stepped outside the car and instantly found himself overcome by the sight of his former school. For six years, he had climbed that flight of steps leading to the grand archway rimmed with gold. Above the entrance, the ostentatious plaque inscribed with the school's logo was now covered by a plastic banner featuring the orphanage's name in Qin characters.

Hao blinked. A dead pigeon lay on its side on the bottom concrete step, its neck coated in dried blood. He stared into its vacant eyes. Before he could kneel to take a closer look, an elderly man and a middle-aged woman in gray robes emerged from the brick building.

They used their voices to greet him, reminding Hao that few citizens had access to Mindbanks in this colony. "What an honor, sir."

Patiently smoothing the front of his red robes, a color reserved for esteemed families of Qin, Hao straightened his back and nodded. "No need to bow," he said calmly. He ascended the steps as the woman scurried past him to dispose of the bird, muttering apologies under her breath. Before she could reach the pigeon, the headmaster had already begun recounting the orphanage's latest achievements.

"Will the Ambassador-Regent be joining us too?" the headmaster asked. Hao shook his head, secretly grateful that he was visiting alone; his anxiety was high enough without his father there. "Of course, that is expected." The headmaster sounded both relieved and disappointed. "I am grateful that you are taking an interest in our charitable cause. Please allow me to show you our humble quarters."

Hao hesitated, briefly wondering if he could avoid the tour entirely, then decided that it wasn't worth inventing an excuse. The headmaster occasionally met with other Party officials—the bleeding hearts who funded Fourth World orphanages such as this one. It was better not to offend this old man, who might bear a grudge for many moons.

I won't be long, Hao informed his driver via Mindbank. He did not bother to check the rose gold watch on his wrist, gifted by a storied Swiss brand hoping to curry favor with his father. He knew that the car would wait for him, no matter how much time he needed.

AS THE HEADMASTER WALKED HIM AROUND THE EMPTY CLASS-rooms where he once attended lectures, Hao learned that fifty students were now crammed into each lecture space rather than the eighteen who used to nap through classes. When they entered what had been his first homeroom, his fingers caressed the underside of an old desk, searching for initials carved into the wood long ago. What had she written there for him to read?

He felt a stab of frustration at his inability to remember, ruing the absence of Mindbanks then. It had been a long time since he had truly forgotten anything. Before leaving, the assistant guided them to the former teacher offices, now converted into dormitories, each with three bunk beds and an empty patch of floor for the orphans to store their belongings. Later, when the headmaster escorted him to what used to be the gender-neutral restroom, he recalled once finding a full pack of cigarettes floating in the toilet bowl and wondering whom it might have belonged to. The tiled restroom was now almost unrecognizable, transformed into a second pantry to accommodate all the extra mouths.

"Of course, you can remember perfectly, what every room used to be," the headmaster said, staring longingly at the scar along the boy's temple. Few in Qin had the clearance to own a Mindbank prototype, much less in a colony; had it not been for his father, Hao would never have been granted such a privilege. The headmaster must have assumed that Hao had been accessing memories via his device, when his nostalgia had been enough to recall almost everything.

"Is it always so quiet here?" Hao asked, finding the empty hallways unnerving.

The headmaster shook his head. "In honor of your visit, we sent most of the orphans on a field trip to the New Arlington Cemeteries. We worried that your tour might otherwise suffer, that the building would be too crowded." The old man then gestured toward a row of unused lockers ahead and lamented that funding shortfalls made it impossible for the school to hire sufficient staff to conduct contraband checks. "Of course, if the Ambassador-Regent could provide us with more resources, we could do more for the children . . ."

Galled by the man's shamelessness, especially given how much his father had already donated, Hao picked up his pace. Upon reaching the staircase, he finally inquired about the request he'd made prior to his visit. With an obsequious grin, the headmaster assured him that everything had been set up in the Hall of Filial Piety.

"I believe it was called the Montgomery Room," the headmaster added.

"She will be there then?" Hao asked. Then he bolted up the stairs before the old man could respond. In truth, his fears ran deeper.

Will she even remember me?

STANDING BEFORE THE HALL, HAO STOPPED AND THANKED THE headmaster for the tour. The old man bowed, but the boy did not notice, too distracted by the open door. For years, he had idled away hours after school in that room. Vague images of his messy handwriting on practice papers drifted into his natural memory, but he quickly pushed the recollections away.

He took a breath and entered. As his eyes adjusted to the dim light, he was surprised to find the room nearly exactly as he remembered—the same wooden tables and chairs, mosaic tiles on the floor. Faded squares on the oak walls hinted at where oil paintings of deceased American-white headmasters used to hang. Then, sitting behind one of the tables in the center of the room—there she was.

Jill.

The girl waved and gave him a terse smile. She was dressed in a gray robe, similar to what the headmaster's assistant had worn. Thick blond hair flowed over her shoulders, longer than he remembered. The sleeves looked short. He wondered if the robes belonged to her, or whether the administrators had dressed her up in advance of his visit.

On the dark wooden table before her lay a chessboard; only instead of the Western variant, she had set up a game of Qin chess. Rather than sixty-four squares, the board consisted of a nine-by-ten grid with flat red and black discs positioned at symmetrical intersections. Each disc had its rank printed with a Qin character: Soldier, Cannon, Chariot, Elephant, Horse, Guard, General.

Hao shuffled across the room and sank into the chair across

from her. Three years had passed; he was sure that he looked different too. Certainly he had not worn robes the last time he attended this school; that fashion had been instituted after the War to promote Qin patriotism and its proudly unbroken history as a nation. Out of habit, the boy touched the side of his face where his glasses once pressed before the minor medical procedure that had eliminated the need for them.

Should he offer her a hug? Did she expect one?

He decided to play a move instead. As his right hand hovered above a Cannon, his billowing sleeve covered half of the board. He withdrew his arm to see the pieces more clearly.

"You look good in red," the girl said. "Now, if you only played half as good, then maybe I won't kick your ass at this game."

Hao froze, sleeves half-rolled. It had been years since anyone dared to use such language with him. And in English, no less! He felt the tension on his face soften.

"Jill."

"You just remembered? All that time in Qin make you slow?" She tapped on the board to hurry him. He pushed one of the red Cannons toward the center.

"Maybe it's your hair? Or the acne scars?"

She pulled her hair into a ponytail, then laughed. The sound was throatier than he remembered. Looking more closely, he noticed a narrow swath of skin on her neck, just above the gray robes, that was darker than the rest of her face. Were they burns? Maybe the light was playing tricks on his eyes; he did not want to imagine what she had endured during the War. Before the Americans surrendered, there were rumors that they had ruthlessly set fire to some of their own cities, to eliminate buildings of strategic significance that the Qin military might occupy. Perhaps she had been caught in the crossfire during an American retreat. It was easier for him to believe this, to blame the US rather than any soldiers from Qin.

He knew that the only way to get the truth was to ask her.

Before he could gather his courage, Jill mirrored his move by dragging her Cannon to the center. "You been practicing?" she asked. "You better have been practicing. Or have you been getting drunk on baijiu instead? With your new friends?"

Hao shook his head. "To be honest, none of my friends in Qin play—"

"Because they don't want to offend the Ambassador-Regent's son by winning?"

He smiled nervously, as he advanced his Horse from the back rank.

"No. What I was going to say was—" He tapped his right temple. "Anyone who played and was connected enough to buy a Mindbank started downloading memories from professionals, even grandmasters. That took the fun right out of the game."

"I bet." She paired her Elephants, a defensive maneuver. "Sounds fancy."

Hao was glad that she did not ask if he was cheating with his Mindbank now, although had she understood the technology, she would've noticed that his eyes were still focused on her face rather than glazed over. His hand lingered over his advanced Horse to make sure that he wasn't falling into a trap. He felt disoriented speaking in English. It was odd of Jill to pair her Elephants so early. Usually, she did not move her Guards or Elephants unless she perceived an imminent threat against her General.

"How's your Ba?" she asked. "Everything all right?"

"Oh, he hasn't been home much. Mostly traveling." He shrugged. "It's the job. He's not just the ambassador anymore. Most meetings are held via Mindbank, but he's also been putting in the kilometers." He advanced his other Horse, choosing a safe move because he wasn't sure what else to play.

She immediately pushed one of her Soldiers toward the River

that split the board in half. Hao cautioned himself to play more slowly. If her Soldier managed to cross the River, it would be able to capture pieces sideways. He needed to attack, but at the right time.

"Aren't you going to ask about my dad too?" the girl asked.

When he met her gaze, Hao was reminded of the green flecks in her eyes. "I'm so sorry, Jill. I wish—"

"I'm kidding." She gave a curt laugh that died in her throat. "I wanted to see what you'd say."

"My father considered him a friend. But the War was chaotic. Finding you alone was a miracle—"

"I said I was kidding!" She tapped the board. "If you don't hurry up and move, the headmaster's going to worry that I offed you."

Hao opened his mouth to ask about her life at school, then stopped himself. He had toured the classrooms. What did he expect her to say?

"Do I have to hunt for a clock? Have you forgotten how to play?"

Tensing his jaw, he moved his Chariot to prepare an attack.

EIGHT YEARS AGO, JILL HAD INITIALLY IGNORED THE BOY WHO came to her house. He had been accompanied by his father, a stern man with military posture in an impeccably tailored suit. The physical contrast between them had been jarring—while the faint outline of muscles was visible beneath the man's dress shirt, his son was scrawny, with long arms that reminded her of a monkey she had seen on a zoo trip. Across his face, the boy wore dark frames that made his pupils look small. After her father introduced the pair as the new Chinese ambassador and his son, Jill groaned; she knew that soon enough her father would ask her to welcome the boy into her school, as she had done twice before as a favor for the children of other dignitaries.

Could the boy even speak English? What were the odds that he was smart? Jill loathed the privileged kids at her school, especially foreign ones, even though she knew that she might not have gotten in either without her father's connections to the State Department.

"Rest assured, Emily and I will see to it that the little guy has no trouble starting in the fall," her father told the ambassador as they sat around the dining table. "I've smoothed out a couple of visa issues for the school's teachers. I can't imagine them raising any objections."

He laughed loudly, even though nobody else joined in. Both the Chinese boy and his father politely sipped on their tea. Her mother watched on anxiously. Jill hated that her father made her mother entertain guests, forcing her to wear pearls and too much makeup. It was summer! Why weren't they on vacation? Didn't anyone have anything better to do than drink tea and talk politics?

"Our little angel, Jill—she'll make sure that Hao feels at home, won't she?" her father said cheerfully, gesturing toward her end of the table.

She scowled. Enough. Without a word, she rose to her feet and walked toward the stairs. Behind her, she heard her father raising his voice in warning and the ambassador making excuses on her behalf—something about her "free spirit" and how his son could learn from her.

In her room, Jill sprawled across the bed. It wasn't her fault that she didn't want to spend every weekend entertaining her father's guests. That was his job! She buried her face in the sheets and wished that she didn't care so much about upsetting him. Maybe she shouldn't have left the table so abruptly; she would surely be grounded as soon as the Chinese guests left.

Jill groaned and tried to ignore the voices downstairs. Although she liked their home in Bethesda, the brownstone's floorboards were surprisingly thin. She wouldn't be surprised if there were a colony of termites living in their walls. Gloria, their housekeeper, was so old that she probably wouldn't notice if one crawled in front of her nose. Part of Jill hoped that Gloria would come to check on her, but the housekeeper was probably busy preparing sandwiches for the guests. Springing from the bed, Jill walked over to her laptop and clicked Play on one of the playlists recommended by Spotify.

Soon, the mellow tones of a grand piano filled her room, its rhythms transporting her to a calmer state of mind.

Chopin? Beethoven? She did not care, so long as it drowned out the noise. Grabbing a chess book from the shelf, Jill returned to bed and tried to follow one of the games. She had nearly dozed off when she heard footsteps on the stairs. Maybe her father was bringing the guests upstairs to show off his watch collection; she rolled her eyes and listened more carefully. The grown-ups were still in conversation downstairs, so it had to be the boy. Lowering the volume with her phone, she pressed her stomach snugly against the mattress and pretended to read until she heard a faint noise near her doorway.

"Are you just going to stand there and stare?"

Turning her head, she saw surprise flicker across the boy's face. She wondered whether it was partly her voice, its unnaturally high pitch, that had alarmed him. At school, Jill usually depressed her voice, speaking one octave lower so that her teachers wouldn't assume that she was a dumb blonde, but she rarely bothered to make such adjustments at home.

"Come in already." She waved her arm, as if to show off the room. Light streamed in from the window, illuminating the bookcases on each wall. Nobody could think that she was stupid, given the books in her room. Maybe the boy could relieve her boredom; she patted the empty spot beside her.

"Do you like to read?" she asked. "What do you read? My friends all like to read."

The boy hesitantly sat beside her on the bed. "I don't know that one," he said, pointing at the pink cover between her fingers.

His accent wasn't bad; he had clearly studied English before. "This?" Jill raised the book, then lowered it. "Classic. Dvoretsky and Yusupov, 1996."

When the boy confessed that the only Russian writers he had

heard of were Tolstoy and Chekhov, she chuckled. "Oh, I hadn't heard of these two either. *Positional Play*. It's a book about chess. Can you play? Look." Flipping the book open to a random page, she pointed at one of the games, giving him time to admire the miniature eight-by-eight grid filled by horses, crowns, and other pictographs of chess pieces.

"Lame, I know. So what? I really get into things. When did being a nerd become a crime?" She turned her attention back to analyzing the game in the book, even as she observed the shy boy from the corner of her eye.

Just as she was getting bored, he spoke again, "Why do you like Baroque music?"

"Oh. Is that what's playing?"

He flicked his fingers in the air as if practicing scales on an invisible keyboard, then nodded. She wondered if he was one of those Chinese kids who wore tuxedos and performed free concerts in the DC shopping malls. "This is Bach."

"Nice. I wish I knew more. Neither of my parents are into music."

The boy nodded again. "Mother," he said. "In China, she play in big concert piano hall—"

"Whoa, that's cool!" Jill blurted. Almost all the wives of her father's guests were stay-at-home moms, and she hated that her mother was no exception. "I'd love to meet her. A real concert pianist."

"Last year, sorry." The boy hesitated. "Last year, she get very sick."

"Oh." Jill squeezed her lips, wishing that she had kept quiet. "Stupid me." She was grateful that her father wasn't present to witness her embarrassment. "I'm sorry."

"It is why we are in America now, after she gone. New life, no problem." The boy pointed at her book. "Can you teach me?"

Jill gently gestured for him to lean in, so that he could more clearly see the pages. If this boy could forgive her faux pas, perhaps they could become friends after all. She began by teaching him everything about Pawns and Queens. How they moved. How a Pawn could transform into a Queen upon promotion, but not vice versa. They were her two favorite pieces, Jill told him, even though she never used them well during competitions.

Years later, he would ask her why she liked those pieces above all others.

"Do we ever really understand why we love something, Hao?" she teased cryptically. Even though she had never considered the question before.

THEIR FIRST MATCH ENDED IN HIS FAVOR, MORE EASILY THAN HE had expected. Unlike the Western variant, where games often ended in closed positions, Qin chess was more tactical. The board was larger and more open, benefiting aggressive players. By contrast, Hao thrived in claustrophobic positions. He was more comfortable grinding out games that left both players with little more than Kings and Pawns by the end.

"Good game." He stuck out his hand; she shook it coolly. "I didn't expect you to play so conservatively," he admitted. "I don't think I've ever seen you move your Elephants or Guards so early."

Jill shrugged as she began resetting the board.

"You didn't let me win, right?" Hao joked, rubbing his neck. When she didn't answer, he raised his left hand in protest, briefly blinding her with the reflection from his watch. "No, we should play the other game too. For old times' sake."

"Sure." As she stood, he could not help but notice how she had grown. His friend had always been tall, but he was surprised that he had not gained any height on her over the past three years. As she turned to search for the Western chess set, he saw that the burn on her neck extended to her back. Did she have more scars, hidden beneath the robes?

"Here you go." She threw the wooden box of pieces haphazardly in his direction, not flinching at the loud crack it made against the table. It had been years since he had seen an international chess set, much less the old-school set they used to play with. As she unrolled the green-and-white-squared vinyl board, Hao gently removed the pieces from the box. The black were sculpted from ebony and the white from boxwood. He enjoyed the familiar heft of each piece in his hand. Despite the chipped edges, they felt the same as when he first began to study the game.

Once more, he wondered about the best way to ask her about the War, how she had survived after her parents were imprisoned, before his father's men discovered her and brought her to the orphanage. He felt a lump in his throat, unable to decide.

"Play white," he offered. "I went first in Qin chess."

"Isn't that a little on the nose?"

He smiled, shrugging. The movement felt odd for his shoulders, too casual, almost foreign. From the board, he scooped up two Pawns, one black and one white, and held them in each fist behind his back. "Choose."

She picked the hand with the black Pawn, then cursed.

JILL REMEMBERED THE LAST TIME THEY WERE TOGETHER IN HER bedroom.

On several occasions, he'd tried to explain why he was flying to Qin the next morning, but she had refused to listen, knowing that there was no way Hao could disobey his father and stay with her in America. Better not show him how upset she was, she told herself, even as she struggled to imagine school without him. For the first time in years, Jill would need to ask someone else to be her lab partner. The next time she worried about an exam, or her father's safety whenever he traveled abroad on behalf of the government, whom would she confide in?

Hao had been her person, the one she'd relied on through the good times and bad—and soon he would be gone. Did he even care that he was about to abandon her?

Out of frustration, Jill had insisted they spend their final hours together playing chess.

It's easier to replace a chess partner than a best friend, she told herself. Nevertheless, during their games, Hao kept trying to circle their conversation back to his imminent departure.

"Grow up," she replied, exasperated. "You're not a citizen here. It's not your fault. Stop pretending that this war isn't going to happen. We're not kids anymore."

"I'll come back," Hao said with a quiver in his voice.

She scoffed and moved to trade Bishops. She recognized that it wasn't the smartest play, but at that moment, she didn't have the patience to manage the closed position on the board.

"Stop." When he placed a hand on her arm, she flinched in surprise.

What did he think he was doing! She shrugged him off. Did he feel sorry for her? Why couldn't he just play?

"You're attacking too hard, Jill," he said gently.

"Too much," she snapped. "You can attack too quickly. And too much. But not too hard." Even as the words escaped her mouth, she was aware of her tone; she had always been patient with his grammar before. Quietly, the boy captured her Bishop with his Knight using the same hand with which he had touched her. On his next move, he pushed a Pawn to create an outpost for his Knight. She cursed loudly, her voice reverberating in the bedroom.

"Don't forget who taught you this game," she warned. She pulled on her ponytail in frustration. Was this really going to be their goodbye? This pathetic game?

Hao kept his eyes fixed on the board as if afraid to meet her gaze. "I'll never forget," he said. Then in one swift motion, he tipped over his King. "Never forget you."

Jill righted it immediately.

"Play!" she yelled. "I don't want charity. Where do you see that I've lost? Where?"

The boy's face reddened as Jill wrapped her fingers around her Queen. As much as she did not want him to leave, she did not want him to remember her as weak in their final moments together. Then, turning away from the board, she allowed her face to soften. For a heartbeat, she dared to hope that everything would turn out all right, that one day he'd return as promised.

AS HAO PONDERED HIS NEXT MOVE, HE WONDERED WHY THIS game should feel any different from the thousands they had played in the past. He had been in this position as white countless times, opening with the Ruy Lopez before castling and reinforcing his Pawns. So why did this game with her feel so painful?

For three years, he had longed to see her again. Where was the girl who taught him so much when he first arrived in this country, a boy mourning his mother without the language to communicate his grief? Where was the girl who once saved him?

Then the question came out of his mouth, its arrival as unexpected as it was inevitable if the two of them were ever to rebuild their relationship.

"Jill, will you return to Qin with me?"

Hao released the horse from his hand. Suddenly, he wondered if that was the real reason why he had traveled twelve thousand kilometers, to ask that question and hear her answer. For the first time in years, he no longer felt like the son of an Ambassador-Regent, beholden to no one save his father, but rather a simple boy with an extraordinary ask.

"Will you come home with me? Live with us in Qin?"

He held his breath. "Please," he added. "Answer me. Jill?"

But no matter how many times he repeated her name, she refused to speak. She pretended to play instead, pushing her pieces around the board in cold anger, then pulling them back to their former positions. In that moment, she hated him for his ignorance, the privilege in his stubborn refusal to recognize that nothing could be the same between them again.

In the quiet room, the ticking of the boy's watch became deafening. She needed only a glance to tell that its case was made of pink gold, the dial revealing itself to be a calendar. Her father had once taught her that the most advanced calendars were called perpetuals for their ability to account for leap years; he used to call them his grail watches, placing his name on the waitlist in every Patek boutique he passed during his travels.

Did Hao know that she would immediately recognize its value? The idea that he would bring something so ostentatious to flaunt before her, knowing that she had nothing left to her name, made her stomach turn. She gritted her teeth, refusing to show any weakness.

Before any answer, she wanted to beat him first. Here. At this game. Staring at the sixty-four checkered squares, she willed her mind to find a better move. The perfect move, if such a thing still existed in the universe.

The boy can wait, she thought bitterly. Let him wait.

THE ISLANDER

Dear Qin citizen, do not open your beautiful eyes.

For the next minute, listen to my voice as we prepare you for your upcoming experience. Understand that this will not resemble other memories you have purchased for your Mindbank. Soon, we will permit you into the body of our hero, to witness the world from his perspective and live out the struggles he faced—but this time, let us invite you into the production of our Memory Epic too.

Give us a moment to calibrate your device. Perfect, the Producer has given us the green light to proceed. We are confident that your Mindbank has the processing power to optimally deliver this memory experience. Please relax, gently open your eyes, and join us when ready.

Now, allow me to begin this story as if it were an American-white fairy tale . . .

ONCE UPON A TIME, THERE WAS A MAN WHO ABANDONED HIS island to save his wife's life. He tried to achieve this by selling his most valuable possession, one that held little value for him and yet might fetch significant coin on the mainland. Of course, he would have preferred that his treasure were a pearl, some tangible symbol of wealth from the ocean that he could hold between his callused fingers and show off to his neighbors. But men of humble birth can hardly expect to choose the nature of their riches. Our hero is no exception.

If this story were a parable, our hero would likely suffer some ignoble end as punishment for his moral failings. But this story will not be a parable, our Producer says. The Qin audience needs no reminders of scorpions lying in wait. Let us make the tale thrilling instead of tragic.

The Producer is a rich man, so my team and I listen intently. Yes, we can edit the islander's memories into a thriller. Yes, we can try to fulfill the Producer's every request.

I encourage my team to smile and bite our tongues in the studio. We have no room to offend our benefactor. How else do you imagine that we artisans of Memory Epics can bring such stories to life for you, our audience?

OUR HERO'S STORY BEGINS BEFORE THE ERA OF MINDBANKS, THE spinning drives in our temples that flawlessly record our memories. To be precise, it takes place during the period when the devices were first introduced, when only the wealthiest in Qin could afford to relive the memories of strangers. Back when it was still rare for ambulance workers transporting bodies to the morgue to secretly extract the past from deceased citizens, downloading their memories to be delivered to the Towers for the entertainment of our most privileged.

Only on the island does the Mindbank remain a myth.

What need did islanders have for such technology, given their paradise of natural riches? Thick rainforests blanket the ground, hibiscus blooming under every tree. With each step, our hero passes another banyan, its limbs reaching toward the sun. Monkeys scurry along the branches with surefooted confidence, obscured from below by the brilliant sunlight.

If trees were sentient, how would they judge our race? But that is a quandary our hero has never considered, for he has always seen himself as a simple man, the insignificant manager of a humble hostel. Unlike others, he never had any interest in visiting the wealthy nations from which his guests came, perpetually in search of rest and relaxation. Yet, since the start of the War, the hostel has not entertained a single guest, not even tourists from Ri-Ben.

"Be patient, my love," his wife says. "Do not worry. The War will soon be over."

On the eve of the Incineration, clasp her hand as you sit beside her atop the terrace roof of the hostel, enjoying the sunset on wooden chairs our hero carved himself. Stare through this man's eyes at the radiant orb descending on the distant silhouettes of Qin skyscrapers. It is a miracle that their island has maintained its independence so far, given the sliver of blue that separates it from the mainland.

How can he not worry? Since the Qin empire began its global military campaign, every nation in the Pacific has fallen along its path, not to mention the powerful Western nations across the ocean whose militaries seem to be faltering.

"Feel these strong kicks from our son in my belly," his wife says, reminding him of their good fortune. "Soon, our family will grow." The man grunts, preoccupied with the survival of his business. His wife squeezes his wrinkled hand. Does he even notice her brave attempts at cheer? Or the sweat dripping down her sunburnt face?

The Incineration will occur the next day. This is a pivotal scene, so shall I ask my assistant, Fang, to adjust the sunlight filters? How about dialing up the background sounds? Please wait a moment as our team discusses how best to escalate the suspense of what is to come.

DEAR QIN AUDIENCE. THE WORLD MUST APPEAR STRANGE AS YOU peer through our hero's eyes. Your eyes now.

Look up, islander. It's the Incineration. It's happening right above us.

Listen to the explosions erupting only a few hundred kilometers away on Ri-Ben. Release a sigh of relief that the Qin missiles did not target your island, or one of your neighbors. So long as the War ends and your guests return, should it matter who wins? Let them own Tai-Wan. Let them own America and the white men walking on those foreign lands.

Marvel at the mushroom cloud billowing in the distance. Mutter a quick prayer. Then run. For as you lift your head and stare at the ferocious haze above, can you not see that winged monstrosity hurtling from the clouds?

Run and don't look back. Not even when you find yourself underneath the shadow of the jumbo jet that will shroud your island in darkness. Run before its silver snout collides with the earth, before the plane explodes into a million shards of metal, engulfing everything in heat.

Run. Before the whole world turns black, as if to signal the end of a scene, a lowering of curtains so that you, our audience, may take a breath to recover.

MAKE IT MORE EXCITING, THE PRODUCER SAYS. MAKE THE ACTION sing louder.

Naturally, I wait for him to finish before expressing my opinions; I have been in this business long enough to know to let the wealthy man share his ideas first.

Can we slow the plane's descent? Before it erupts in flames? the Producer asks.

I nod vigorously. So what if his idea is clichéd? As long as he pays us artisans on time and ensures our good standing with the Party, why should my opinions interfere? It is miraculous enough that I found a Producer willing to support this Memory Epic with references to Ri-Ben, the historical enemy of Qin. He must have faith that our product will be a high-grossing masterpiece capable of stimulating our economy, an outcome always appreciated by our Party.

It is my first time working with this Producer. He is rumored to be related to high-ranking Party officials, so I send his orders down the line. How can I call myself their leader if I do not look out for my creative crew above all other considerations?

Please accept my regrets. Of course my loyalty cannot belong to the audience alone.

THERE IS ONLY ONE HOSPITAL ON THE ISLAND, MORE OF A CLINIC financed by Ri-Ben to serve their tourists. It is dumb luck that the building finds itself unscathed by the plane crash; further luck that our hero finds transport there after pulling his unconscious wife from the wreckage of their home, the charred rubble that once represented their livelihood.

Shall we fast-forward past the blood and gore of the hospital? Just as we've sped through the trauma of our hero seeing his home destroyed, the blood streaming down his wife's face. Shall we muffle the screams, the screech of gurneys? These are the choices we make to prevent the Censors from attaching any content warnings, so this Epic has a chance to reach the wide audience it deserves.

All the beds are occupied by the time our hero arrives. But as every Fourth Worlder knows, everything has a price. So when the Doctor examines the wife's injuries and names an exorbitant sum, our hero agrees without hesitation.

Relax, dear audience. Allow the Doctor a moment to revel in his imaginary profits and ask his nurse to retrieve an extra rollaway. Before long, the wife lies on the bed with a peaceful expression on her face, on morphine and oblivious to the chaos that surrounds them. Breathe a sigh of relief, even if you have already realized that our hero is doomed—since what wealth he possessed has disintegrated into little more than rubble.

For the next three days, our hero silently sits on the bloodstained floor beside her bed, trying to accept that their baby is lost and his wife may never awaken. Fast-forwarding, our hero grieves not only for what he has lost, but also for the moment when his inability to pay the hospital will come to light. What will happen to his wife then? Immerse yourself in his despair.

The Producer finds this scene moving, so I ask Fang to send it to post-production.

All of us in the studio pray in secret that the Qin critics will not find the scene emotionally manipulative and penalize us during awards season.

"ONE WEEK," THE DOCTOR SAYS COOLLY. "IF YOU DO NOT FIND the money, I will throw her out of the ward myself." Although the man has already earned a fortune from this disaster, he has no empathy for our hero, furious that he wasted a rollaway bed on someone unable to pay.

Remember, this story is no parable. It is only a memory, so we cannot punish him.

Bear witness through our hero's eyes; stare at the dried blood along the floor. Listen to the fans thrumming above, passing the stench of death between rooms. Embrace his helplessness.

Even if the hostel had not burned, he would still have been unable to pay the Doctor's price. What choice did he have but to lie? What else could he have done to save her?

"Wait, you were standing near the crash when it happened, right?" the Doctor asks, his voice suddenly calm. "When the plane tumbled from the sky?"

Our hero nods.

"I mean, with your own eyes. Did you see the plane fall?"

Our hero only wishes that he could forget.

"We may be in luck then." The Doctor smirks. "A couple of days ago, a few men from Qin came to the clinic. They asked if we knew anyone who had witnessed the entire incident. Apparently, their boss is willing to pay significant coin. For the right memories."

Memories? Only then does our hero recall the rumors of the mysterious innovations on the mainland, devices capable of extracting a person's past.

Were the stories true? Was such technology real?

One day our hero may learn of wealthy Qin citizens paying exorbitant coin to download and relive the most revolting crimes, from the perspective of defendants and victims alike, in service of their sexual desires. But at this moment, all he cares about is the stranger on the mainland who might pay him enough for memories of the plane crash to save his wife.

How will he get across the water? The harbor has been closed since the beginning of the War. Not even the island gangs operate boats anymore for fear of the Qin coast guard.

"That's not my problem," the Doctor says. "Just take down the hospital's phone number. Oh, if you do get across, ask to speak to the Merchant—"

THE MERCHANT! DID I HEAR THAT RIGHT? THE PRODUCER ASKS. Did we not agree to cut the crime boss from the narrative? Are you trying to get the Censors to reject our Memory Epic?

In the amorphous digital space between our minds, I make my avatar bow in the direction of the Producer's form. How many times did we need to have this debate? Thankfully, we are conducting this conversation via Mindbank; otherwise, it would be impossible for me to hide my frustration, to blame my avatar's expressions on a glitch or processing lag on the Cloud.

Reminding the Producer that our islander's original memories had been sourced from the Merchant's trial, I explain that it would be impossible for us to eliminate the Merchant from our Epic. Moreover, how else would we explain the islander risking his life to cross the ocean? The story wouldn't make sense.

The Producer's avatar scoffs.

I reassure him that we will not glorify the Merchant or his crimes.

Our Epic needs to promote good Qin values, the Producer says. Otherwise, the entire project may be placed in jeopardy.

Thank you for the feedback, I tell him. In the studio, we artisans can get caught up in the minutiae of our stories and lose sight of the bigger picture.

To my surprise, these words make the Producer's avatar cheeks flush red. I did not expect such a reaction, assuming wealthy men must often receive such obsequious praise.

I hope that I haven't interfered too much with the magic of this Memory Epic, he says graciously. One cannot be too careful when it comes to the Censors. But you know that.

I smile. Perhaps I had been too quick to judge the man's capitalistic tendencies.

DEAR AUDIENCE, FORGIVE THE ICY SPRAY HITTING YOUR FACE, the unrelenting wind piercing your cheeks as we rejoin our hero on his journey. You are alive. We fast-forwarded through our hero's memories to save you from the trauma experienced by your body as it nearly shut down for good. The worst is over.

Stop thrashing like a fish out of water. Accept that you are alive due to sheer luck and allow the strangers around you to swaddle your drenched body in blankets. Take time to warm up. You are no longer in the freezing water, fighting to keep your head above the waves as you float toward the mainland. If not for that rainbow beach ball you clung to, abandoned by some hostel guest, you would have drowned long ago. Not only because the ball helped you stay afloat but also because its vibrant colors allowed a Qin coast guard vessel to spot you from a great distance.

Have the blankets given you enough warmth to melt your tongue? To call his name?

"The Merchant!" you scream. There is so much adrenaline flowing through your veins that your words fail to sound coherent, even to your ears. "The Merchant!"

Ocean foam rises and falls behind you, dissipating across both sides of the small boat.

Boat! The half dozen men aboard stare at you blankly, their uniforms identifying them as the Qin coast guard. They were the ones who saved you, yes. Wait for your teeth to slow their clattering, for your senses to return before you try to use your voice again.

Be grateful that the seamen saved you, even if they did so out of curiosity rather than kindness. Wouldn't the sight of a grown man trying to use a rainbow ball to cross a violent strait seem absurd to you too?

You're alive. Let them enjoy a laugh at your expense.

At last, your tongue warms enough to try again. "The Merchant! Take me to the Merchant!" It is your good fortune that they comprehend your dialect, even more so that the man whose name you speak aloud is well regarded for compensating the coast guard handsomely for their cooperation.

The men on the boat argue, pointing fingers in your direction as they discuss what to do. Then, one of them places a hand on your back as you continue to shiver beneath the blankets. Pay no heed to the aches in your body, the growing fear that your numb fingers and toes may never be able to feel sensations again: look up and thank the man with your gaze. Pray that your good fortune has not yet run its course.

WHEN I DISCOVER THAT THE CENSORS HAVE REJECTED THE FIRST cut of our Epic, I nearly break down in the studio. Before we started, the Producer assured us that the Party had granted us preliminary approval; if the Censors could still send back our project, what was the point?

Clearly, I had put too much faith in our Producer's rumored ties to the Party, that his connections would push our project through no matter what. Could I even guarantee the safety of my crew? We would not be the first memory artisans to be sent to reeducation camps for creating unpatriotic content, given the blurred lines of what constitutes moral propriety. Our families could be dishonored in public, our personal memories confiscated for storage inside the Criminal Archives.

My Mindbank pings with a call from the Producer; unable to face him alone, I add my studio crew to the conversation. He is livid, of course. Even the nostrils of his avatar are flared.

At last, he asks one question: Can we save this?

For a while, I say nothing, even as every avatar stares in my direction. In the history of Memory Epics, has any project ever been approved following a first-cut rejection?

Still, I refuse to give up on our dream.

I tell the Producer a rumor I once heard in passing, that a truly extraordinary Memory Epic could bypass the Censors if it received an innovation exemption from the Party.

Promising, the Producer replies, then hesitates. But what kind of innovation would qualify?

The room falls silent as each of us wonders how we could innovate on a storytelling medium as tried and true as memories.

THE ISLANDER AWAITS THE MERCHANT BENEATH A GLASS DOME.
Follow our hero's gaze as it wanders across the room, its endless collection of bounded parchments meticulously arranged along wooden shelves. The scale of the cavernous space overcomes him. In his estimation, it is larger than every room in his hostel combined, including the terrace. Above him, the curved glass is stained with different colors to form a kaleidoscope of images he does not recognize. Lowering his eyes, our hero discovers that he is too afraid to

walk over to the shelves and touch any of the books, for fear that they might crumble upon contact with his coarse hands.

"I hope I did not look as wide-eyed as you when I first came to the mainland."

The Merchant's words echo. Before he can turn toward the voice, the islander is stunned, never having been in a room large enough to produce such reverberations. Was there something wrong with his ears? Or was the soaring ceiling of colors responsible for the repeating sounds? His eyes become transfixed again by the beauty of the dome, its magnificent architecture.

"Marvelous, isn't it? This library used to be the crown jewel of the Qin system," the Merchant says with a chuckle. "Long after books became obsolete, this room remained open to the public, so the Party most certainly shared your admiration."

Shifting his gaze, our hero sees the Merchant for the first time and gasps. Never has he witnessed a man of such stature, the width and height of his enormous physique dwarfing the two Qin bodyguards standing at the library entrance. Uncertain how to react, our islander bows in the manner of the Ri-Ben guests he once entertained, his mind racing.

Did the Merchant live in this building? On the island, our hero had seen certain hotels stacking books onto shelves for tourists—but never has he seen such a grand collection.

Is this the breadth of all Qin knowledge? he asks.

The giant laughs. A moment passes before our hero realizes that the Merchant does not speak through a translator. How can the man understand the island dialect?

Confidently, the Merchant strolls across the hall, clothed only in a loose shirt and shorts.

"It has been a long time since I've talked face-to-face with someone from my birthplace," he explains, placing a hand on the back of his fellow islander. "Perhaps now you can understand my interest in what happened to our home."

Our hero lifts his eyes cautiously to meet the giant's gaze.

"Tell me about the explosion," the Merchant says. "Do not leave anything out, my friend."

DEAR AUDIENCE, WHAT IF WE ABANDONED THIS MEMORY EPIC and left the ending to your imagination? What if I told you that stopping here was one innovation that our crew considered to qualify for the exemption? After all, how many stories from your life truly ended in some neat resolution?

Doesn't our hero deserve a happy ending? Perhaps you can imagine the islander receiving safe passage home, bringing enough coin with him to save his wife. What if I told you that they rebuilt their hostel and went on to raise two beautiful children? A boy and a girl who held their hands, helping their parents in old age to slowly ascend the stone steps of the hostel every night to watch the sunset. What if I told you that the couple died in their sleep on the same starry night, so they never had to live a day without the other? Would you still believe me?

Why open the story with "once upon a time" if our hero's journey does not end like some American-white fairy tale?

IN THE LIBRARY, THE MERCHANT LISTENS ATTENTIVELY.

He sighs at the right moments along our hero's voyage. He places his hand over his heart when our islander describes the instant of collision, when the plane transformed into a fireball upon contact with the earth, the panic of awaking concussed in the smoke. Our hero shares the horror of finding his wife unconscious in the rubble of their burning home, then the long struggle to convince other survivors to help them. The Merchant shakes his head in sympathy when he hears the gruesome state of the clinic following the Incineration. He does not bother asking after the wife's health, since he understands that our hero would not have crossed the strait had she regained consciousness.

Yet when the story is finished, the giant apologizes for his inability to offer any coin in compensation for his fellow islander's ordeal.

"Unfortunately, it is one of my principles that I cannot pay for anything worthless," the Merchant explains. "Sadly, nothing you shared was new. The explosion you described only confirms my theory—that the plane crash was collateral damage from Qin's large-scale military attack on Ri-Ben. I'm sorry. But you wouldn't ask me to compromise on my principles, would you?

"You don't even have a Mindbank I can connect to in order to verify your story!" The giant spreads his arms to gesture at the labyrinth of pages, then throws his head back in cackling laughter. "Trusting your memories would be like flipping open one of these books—and expecting to read the whole truth!"

Had our hero risked his life for nothing? For a long time, he stands beneath the dome, lost in thought. Until he decides that no—he refuses to accept this pathetic end, to allow this giant to dictate all the terms, surrounded by the walls of infinite parchment. No, he cannot go back to the island without the coin to save his wife. And that is when he realizes that the Merchant is wrong, because there is one way for this wealthy man to verify his story.

"Take my memories," our hero demands quietly. "Take all of them and check."

The Merchant smiles, unable to take our islander seriously. "Oh, do you know how much trouble that would bring me? The Party is already investigating my business with the ambulances. There is a reason why we only extract memories from the terminally ill. Go home, my friend. Trust me."

Our hero calmly reminds the Merchant that neither of them are from Qin.

"Why would the Party care about what happens between two

islanders?" he says, knowing the answer. "If you promise to save my wife, I will give you all of my memories. Surely that's worth something. More than enough to satisfy your principles. My entire past can be yours."

Allow the Merchant time to reconsider, as we move into his perspective. Although they have just met, the crime boss is surprised by the fondness he feels for this naïve islander. Even if they can agree on a deal, the Merchant decides that he wants the exchange to be fair. Or at least, for them both to appreciate the full consequences.

"It's true. I may be able to earn a small fortune selling your experiences from the island. Your life would appear exotic to the Party scions who'd bid on and revel in your memories." The Merchant lifts his hand. "Still, you must understand and accept the costs."

Our hero frowns, uncomprehending.

"As I said, there is a reason why we've only been extracting memories from the dying. The technology remains in its infancy. We cannot pick and choose which memories to extract. If I take your memories, you won't be able to get them back." The Merchant's voice softens. "Maybe the technology will evolve, but if you sell me everything today, you won't remember your wife tomorrow, nor recall any reason to return to the island. You may senselessly wander the mainland until you die. Is that worth the gamble that your Doctor can save her? Are you certain enough to sacrifice your remaining time on this Earth?"

The Merchant needs only one look at our hero's face to understand. In the islander's eyes, the giant imagines the depth of our hero's devotion to make such a sacrifice.

"Very well. I accept your proposal."

THAT EVENING, THE OPERATION IS CARRIED OUT. IN THE FINAL seconds before the anesthesia is administered, our hero thinks of his wife. He does not return to their wedding day, nor to the happiest periods of their marriage; instead, he finds himself revisiting memories of reconciliation following their most frivolous fights. As his eyes close, he relishes every moment that they chose to love each other despite their faults. It is this final sensation that our hero enjoys before he loses consciousness, along with his ability to recall any arrangements made in the past.

Thankfully, the Merchant stays true to his word. Because when the giant experiences our hero's memories, he unexpectedly becomes attached to the wife's fate as well. He soon sends his men to compensate the Doctor in full, accompanied by not-so-veiled threats of consequences if she were not to receive the best care. And after the wife miraculously recovers, she is shocked to receive an unmarked envelope with the details of a digital wallet generous enough to rebuild the hostel, without any return address to send her thanks.

So moved is the Merchant by our hero's devotion that he never sells the memories but keeps them in his private vault to experience at his leisure. And that is where our hero's memories remain for many moons, until the Merchant is arrested and convicted by the Qin courts of illegally profiting from the sale of unregulated memory content, and his assets are wholly transferred to the Criminal Archives. Where the memories are stored for many moon-millennia, until they are accessed to produce this Memory Epic.

Rejoice, dear audience. The memories of our hero's sacrifice are forgotten no more.

OUR DEEPEST GRATITUDE TO THE PARTY FOR GRANTING US THE exemption.

Thank you for inspiring this hybrid approach so that we may share our islander's journey alongside our creative struggles. We wish to thank the Censors too. Even if *The Islander* is one day deemed inappropriate for Mindbank consumption, we honor your tireless work to defend the cohesion of our Qin society.

To our Producer, the true genius behind this project. None of this would have been possible without your unparalleled vision and gracious presence in the Memory Epic. I cannot wait to work together in the future. Thank you to the Archives for allowing us to repurpose the islander's memories from the Merchant's trial. Most of all, I want to thank our audience for purchasing this Epic. Know that we take none of your generosity for granted.

Everything we have today, we owe to you and our glorious Party.

FIRST VIRAL MEMORY: *CHANKONABE*

Foreword from the Party

Unless you were a child raised without Mindbanks, disconnected from the rest of our glorious society, you must be familiar with the Memory Epic *Chankonabe*. Released two thousand moons ago, the reunion story of a sumo wrestler and his mother has long been lauded as a classic of Mindbank entertainment. However, the most interesting aspect of the Memory Epic may not have been its celebrated plot but rather the unlikely nature of its rise to popularity, coupled with its role in introducing Mindbanks to ordinary citizens during the technology's commercial infancy.

In fact, early records suggest that when the state-owned enterprise first published *Chankonabe* after the War, few in the organization anticipated that it would remain long in public circulation. For one, the story of the sumo wrestler was set on the island of Ri-Ben, a nation famously incinerated as punishment for its historical crimes against Qin. The idea that our citizens would pay coin to experience the reunion of the protagonist wrestler with his mother was a financial gamble at best. Prior to the Memory Epic's launch, rumors spread that *Chankonabe* might not even pass the review by Censors, who could decide that the plot incited unnecessary sympathy for our nation's former enemies.

Thank goodness the creators were able to convince the Party otherwise! Research suggests the Party had been eager to promote

Memory Epics to Qin citizens after loosening restrictions on Mind-bank ownership. After all, it is believed that many citizens were feeling restless and eager for entertainment following the first outbreak of the Chrysanthemum Virus.

Recall the Memory Epic's quiet opening in a village in Ri-Ben:

> She is a wrinkled woman who lives in a minka with sliding paper
> doors and tatami floors . . . On a wooden stool, she sits and gazes
> at the flame flickering above her rusty stove.

Note the raw emotion that underpins the setting, taking full advantage of the Mindbank's inherent strength in conveying intimacy. Although this approach has become commonplace, Qin audiences of that era were accustomed to large-scale action sequences following generations of "superhero" content imported from Qin-America. Therefore, when audiences resonated so strongly with the opening, many in the industry were surprised, given the Epic's humble and understated nature.

OF ITS MANY INNOVATIONS, *CHANKONABE* IS BEST KNOWN FOR pioneering the Memory Editing concept of layering Mantras atop its central narrative:

> Prepare daikon, kombu, mirin, soy sauce, and red miso paste.
> Stir above a blue flame until the miso paste dissolves.

Recited by the sumo wrestler's elderly mother, the first Mantras consisted of recipe fragments for chankonabe stew, mixed with a sense of urgency imbued by the mother's desire to cook for her son before she loses her sight. This desperation is mirrored in the second narrative, where Mantras of sumo-wrestling rituals were applied to the son's story, cleverly weaving an invisible thread between the protagonists:

> Before any match, the sumo wrestler scatters salt to purify the ring.
> The Shinto religion demands this.
> It is why the gyōji referees dress in the robes of priests.

Historians acknowledge the use of Mantras as critical to the universal adoption of Mindbanks. Prior to *Chankonabe*, the notion that audiences might one day seamlessly shift perspectives between characters in a single Epic appeared to be nothing more than a foolish dream. Indeed, most early adopters of Mindbanks suffered from severe nausea upon embodying a second persona. Thankfully, the Mantras in *Chankonabe* eased new Mindbank adopters through such character transitions, paving the way for thousands of Epics produced over the next hundred moons to feature prominent parallel narratives.

TWO MOON-MILLENNIA AFTER ITS RELEASE, HISTORIANS CONtinue to debate the identities of *Chankonabe*'s creators. Many theorize that the rights to the Memory Epic fully accrued to the state-owned enterprise, which explains why the highly anticipated battles over royalty payments never came to pass. Some suggest that the creators may have been prohibited from going public due to strict nondisclosure agreements. Others argue that the secrecy around *Chankonabe*'s creators may have been a kindness from the state-owned enterprise to protect its employees from scrutiny following the Epic's viral success, given the controversial Ri-Ben setting.

Conspiracy theories also remain popular. How did the business procure the original memories from the sumo wrestler and his mother? Might the creators have had Ri-Ben blood themselves?

Equally fraught has been the debate over why the Epic became so popular. Was it driven by our national curiosity toward Ri-Ben, our hunger for stories about their culture, following the Incineration? The introduction of Mantras? Some have even suggested that the Epic's success was not driven by its exceptional content but by its brilliant advertising strategy during the Cyber 11-11 shopping holiday.

We may never uncover the truth behind these questions, even after *Chankonabe* has become one of the most downloaded memories of all time. Regardless of what you believe, all Qin citizens owe much to its mysterious creators for helping make Mindbanks ubiquitous in our glorious society. Please honor them by experiencing this classic once more.

Whether for the first time or thousandth, the Party welcomes you.

Chankonabe

She is a wrinkled woman living in a minka with sliding paper doors and tatami floors, a half-day's walk from Kunisaki City in Oita Prefecture.

On a wooden stool, she sits and gazes at the flame flickering above her rusty stove. She brushes strands of gray hair behind her ears so that she can more clearly see the fire heating her precious chankonabe, a stew she has not made for many seasons.

Prepare daikon, kombu, mirin, soy sauce, and red miso paste.
Add generously to what soup you have, in your largest pot.
Stir above a blue flame until the miso paste dissolves.

Many summers ago, a little boy in this house called the woman okāsan. But this evening, her son is nowhere to be seen. Beside the stove, the woman reads and rereads every line of the treasured parchment passed down from her own mother, every tiny character written by her okāsan's gentle hand. Although she buried her mother long ago in the nearby hills, the woman dares not alter the recipe, save for adjustments to the quantity of meat to accommodate her son's growth, or at least what she imagines his appetite has become.

Chankonabe nurtures. This stew is eaten by the sumo wrestlers.
It will bring your family warmth and joy.

When the little boy still lived in Oita Prefecture and cut rice stalks with a dull iron scythe by his father's side, his mother would cook chankonabe as a reward, a rare treat after each harvest. The stew was traditionally reserved for sumo wrestlers, too hearty to be a regular meal. The boy cried in delight every time he returned from the fields to smell the fresh chicken broth steaming on the stove, in the joyous moments before their family ate together.

Some nights, when she cannot fall asleep on her mat, the woman prays to the small shrine of Ta-no-Kami, the spirit of abundant rice harvests, standing at the corner of her room. But rather than plentiful rice harvests, she prays for dreams—memories of warmth, the sounds of delight her little boy made when he recognized the scent of chankonabe, and her husband's laugh, rumbling from deep within his belly.

Peel the burdock root under cold water.
Drench your handful of leeks, then cook maitake mushrooms
with oil over high heat.
Mix with broth. Allow to simmer.

Many harvests ago, the woman noticed how the body of her little boy had grown thick, arms hard as rock protruding from a sturdy trunk, the fruits of his labor in the fields. And of course, the bowls of chankonabe.

"When did our boy become so strong?" the woman wondered aloud in the kitchen one day.

Her husband patted her gently on the shoulder. "It is all your credit." Sweet mouth: he was always good at paying her compliments, from the moment their eyes met in their parents' presence to the words he whispered in her ear the night they first made love.

One month later, both men were gone from her life. Like a fog drifting away unseen into distant hills, until nothing was left of them save memories, and regrets.

Kill one whole chicken. One which stands strong upon two legs.

The wrinkled woman slides off a stool, steadying herself despite her failing vision. Gingerly walking to the shed, she picks up a metal scythe from its bed of straw and leaves to slay one of her feathered companions.

THE SUN HAS YET TO RISE, BUT HARU IS ALREADY SCRUBBING THE loincloths of his senpai. His black hair rests atop his head in a chonmage, his loincloth wrapped tightly around his girth to avoid any mishaps during training.

For many hours after, he will not eat breakfast, intent on slowing his metabolism. Compared to a typical Japanese boy, Haru resembles a small mountain, weighing close to two hundred pounds. But relative to the other rikishi, the junior wrestlers in his stable, the boy remains a feather.

To compensate for his failures, Haru seeks to please his oyakata by performing his chores diligently. White bubbles rise in his wooden bucket, making it difficult to see when the clothes become clean. In his head, he repeats his sumo master's mantras in preparation for his training.

Before any match, the sumo wrestler scatters salt to purify the ring.

The Shinto religion demands this.

It is why the gyōji referees dress in the robes of priests.

Haru prefers these mornings in the laundry room. When he is sent instead to the kitchen to prepare the daily chankonabe, all Haru is reminded of—as he chops endless buckets of daikon, mushrooms, bok choy, cabbage, and chicken drumsticks—are his inadequacies.

Not in the ring, but at the dining table. For at seven thirty in the morning, when the senior sekitori wrestlers awake from their slumbers and ready for their morning meals, the rikishi eat alongside them. Yet no matter how many bowls of stew he ingests, Haru cannot match the fervor with which his peers consume to gain weight, not without throwing up before the broth can settle in his stomach.

Rikishi eat ten thousand calories per day.

There is no weight limit in sumo. Eating is your duty.

In his first months after joining the stable, Haru allowed alcohol to become his companion. Washed down with stew, the beer lessened his loneliness and numbed the hurt that ebbed in his chest—the understanding that his parents had sent him away. He drank heavily. Until one evening, the strongest wrestler of their stable laid a hand on the bottle and refused to allow Haru to move it. Only when the boy tried to grab the alcohol repeatedly—when he realized that he had become dependent on it to blunt his longings—did he begin to restrain his consumption. Because of Akebono.

The dining table that morning is devoid of conversation; no topic more important than the calories in front of them. As Haru gulps down another bowl of stew, he revisits memories of his mother's chankonabe. With each swallow, he remembers the daikon they once grew in their fields. With each swallow, he remembers the warmth of home.

FLECKS OF MOISTURE STAIN THE CHEEKS OF THE OLD WOMAN.

Is it the fault of the stockpot? She wipes the water from her cheeks and her wrinkled forehead. Bending over the pot, she fans the soup with her palm.

> Lay pieces of chopped chicken skin-side down in hot oil.
> Cook until browned; otherwise, the meat will stick.

It is true that the decision to send their son away had been her husband's. When his hair began to drop askew on the tatami, the couple had no choice but to accept that change was inevitable. They knew that if the boy learned of his father's illness, he would refuse to leave, knowing that his mother would struggle to run the farm alone. Yet their town was no place for dreamers. Most of the young men had already left to build lives in nearby Kunisaki City, or those metropolises of light the woman had seen on televisions, reachable only by bullet train.

"What future will our son have if he is forced to grow up in these fields, watching his father fade?" her husband lamented. "Who will take care of him once I turn into ash?"

I will, the woman wanted to say. Instead, she stayed silent.

> Taste the broth of the dissolved miso, daikon, and kombu.
> Add soy sauce until the flavors resemble perfection.

The old woman feels her eyes water. Her husband now lies beneath a headstone, name etched into the rock, so she is alone in her guilt.

Stirring the stew with a ladle, she inhales steam rising from the pot. A fragile hope expands in her chest that the flames are why her vision blurs, why the light in her eyes grows dimmer after every moon.

Mada, the old woman says to her shrine. *Not yet.* Some nights, she feels grateful for her disease. It feels appropriate, this dulling of life—a worthy punishment for sending her son away. For years she tried not to resent her husband for leaving her so soon, content to bear her loneliness. Until last month, when she realized that her eyes had deteriorated so much that she might no longer even recognize her son's face. Then, as if a wire in her heart had tripped, she succumbed to the selfish desire to see him one final time, even if it distracted him from his training.

> Do not waste: Remember that your uneaten rice came from the sweat of farmers.
> That it could have been used to brew sake.

This is why she makes chankonabe tonight.

TRAINING COMMENCES AFTER BREAKFAST FOLLOWING A WORD from their oyakata. Haru sweeps the sand floor of the dohyō, preparing the sacred ring. Like the other rikishi, he nurses old injuries, wrapping them with white tape before tightening his loincloth.

Haru begins to stretch. He rocks his mountainous body from side to side in shiko pose, slapping his sides before sinking into deep squats.

> Stamp out evil spirits with your shiko, those who circle your dohyō.
> Do not let them steal your victory.

As the boy performs his daily stretches, he secretly watches Akebono press his head into his knees, flanks rippling. Haru tries to mimic his elder. Although Akebono is only three years older, he has been offered the rank of sekitori.

Why does he deserve such an honor? Merely because he weighs three hundred pounds? Unexpectedly, in silent protest, Haru refuses to close his eyes during the prayer. For a moment, he seeks to rebel—against his elders, the Shinto religion, the parents who set him upon this path.

It is a gift that during training Haru is afforded little time for such foolish thoughts. In the dohyō, he and his fellow rikishi quietly move into their positions. They face off in deep squats as their heads bob above clenched muscles, sweaty backs and chafing loincloths sinking into the quicksand of their bellies. Then, with no more warning than a flick of a wrist, Haru pushes off from the earth and launches toward the wrestler before him.

The deep suck of compressed air on flesh reverberates around the stable when they collide. Breathing in the stench of his opponent's sweat, Haru manages to reach his fingers into the other man's loincloth to yank him off-balance, pushing him out of the ring.

Gasping, Haru bows to his fellow rikishi without emotion.

Exiting the dohyō, he feels his oyakata's gaze on his back. He is careful to bury the pride in his chest, remembering how he once smiled after a victory—and the three violent blows he received as punishment from his master's shinai. That thick slab of bamboo.

Should Haru still be considered a boy, given the pain he has endured? Sometimes, when his head is buried in the flesh of an opponent, he wonders this too.

Yet the answer is obvious. He is only a rikishi, a trainee without permission to sleep outside the stable, not allowed to even form a family of his own. Powerless, however strong he becomes.

THE OLD WOMAN FEELS WET DREAD BUBBLING UP IN HER CHEST as she nears the moment when her stew is fully cooked, and she must leave her place of comfort.

Add chicken thighs, carrots, potatoes, and cabbage to the pot.

Cover until the potatoes become soft. Carefully crack eggs.

When the eggs are poached, she uses her entire body to lift the stockpot off the flame. For a moment, she worries that she will spill the orange stew onto the floor—perhaps then she will have an excuse to abandon her mission—but she takes a deep breath instead, ignoring the ache in her arms to lay the pot gently onto wood.

Do not forget to sprinkle spring onions to enrich the stew, to make the meal memorable.

The next morning, the woman readies to leave. Struggling to fit her best kimono over sloping shoulders, she laments that she never properly beat her boy. Worries fill her head—that her boy may have grown up too weak to bear the pain a sumo wrestler must endure.

Perhaps her kindness had been poison.

So what if neither she nor her husband had been able to hide their tears when the oyakata came to escort their boy to the stable? She had risen to her feet to run after them as soon as her son walked beyond the door; to her surprise, even in his weakened state her husband had been able to hold her back. Together, the couple wept, taking solace in the promise that their boy would not go hungry for at least the next half decade. They reminded each other that their boy would learn rituals, discipline, honor, strength. Then one day, perhaps after he had fought in the dohyō, after he had earned a high rank, he could return to his okāsan. And pay respects to his otōsan.

Or so that is the story the old woman chose to believe for many years as she shut her ears to reports of sumo wrestlers retiring at a young age from injury or diabetes. For so long she had refused to allow her faith to waver in the tales she told to justify her sacrifice. Until the light in her eyes began to fade, and at last, it became impossible to keep lying to herself.

TONIGHT, HARU IS DONE WITH HIS PREPARATIONS.

The boy has accepted that he will never amount to greatness. Eat, train, eat, train, sleep. Repeat. Haru has tired of these routines he did not choose for himself, those brutal blows.

Without the shinai, sumo would not be sumo.

He always had a fondness for summer nights, despite their humidity. For no better reason, he has chosen this evening, when it will not be so cold in the mountains, to leave. He can cover great distances with the stamina he gained from training. Perhaps he can even make it to Osaka Station and sneak onto the bullet train that brought him here so many years ago.

Will he remember where to transfer?

The night before he leaves, Haru hides rice balls underneath a fresh loincloth, meals for the next few days. He will be fine—surely, he can afford to lose a few pounds if the rice runs out. Beyond these stables, he is a giant. Or so he reminds himself.

When Haru cannot sleep, he worries that his okāsan and otōsan might be angry. But soon the harvest will arrive and his strength will be of great help to his family; then they will appreciate his decision to come home. When he first arrived at the stable, he worried that he might never forgive his parents for letting the oyakata take him from their home, but as the years passed, his anger had exhausted its fuel. Instead, the boy allows himself to dream, to long for them.

Perhaps they will even tell him that they were wrong to send him away.

IT IS TIME. HARU LIES ON HIS BACK AND LISTENS TO THE SHALLOW breaths of the sleeping rikishi nearby. Silently, he gathers his belongings, the loincloth filled with rice. Crouching, he creeps past the other wrestlers on the tatami mats, hoping that their snores will hide the sound of his movements.

As Haru crosses the room, the pounding in his chest becomes unbearable; he places one hand on his heart and waits for it to slow. When at last Haru slides open the thin paper door, he is confronted with an unexpected sight—the scowl of his oyakata in the hallway.

"Doko he?" the master asks. "Where are you going?"

Frozen, Haru is saved by the miracle of his body bending at the waist from muscle memory, the instinctive bow hiding the dread across his face.

"RISE, RIKISHI."

All around him, his fellow wrestlers awake from their slumber. Still, Haru dares not lift his eyes, fear paralyzing his body as he hears others murmur in confusion. Never has the oyakata woken them this way. Silent questions permeate the air as the old man leads the ungroomed rikishi to the training quarters, their topknots untied and hair floating in the night wind. Yet no strangeness can compare to the sight of who lies in the center of their dohyō: their most respected sekitori, on the floor, his face ashen—Akebono.

"Do you recognize this man?" the oyakata asks; the rikishi nod.

"DO YOU RECOGNIZE THIS DESERTER?"

Gasps fill the room, then silence, as they each attempt to conceal their shock, their collective shame. Removing the shinai from his belt, the old master brings it down hard onto Akebono's back.

Blood trails along his skin; the mountain opens his mouth in pain, but no words escape.

Akebono. Weeks away from competing in the Tokyo Grand Tournament. On track to becoming an oyakata and forming his own stable. The last wrestler Haru would have expected to run.

"He has dishonored you!" Another smack onto the mountain. A dozen strikes later, the old man has run out of breath, his shinai split into shards. Yet he continues to rain blows upon Akebono's back, until the bamboo turns dark red.

Stop, Haru says. *Stop!* But he shouts this only in his mind. He averts his eyes, understanding that these thoughts alone deserve the shinai . . .

"Why, Akebono?" the master asks, panting.

At last, the sprawled mountain speaks. "Because the future of sumo—is oblivion."

Instinctively, the oyakata raises the shards of bamboo in his hand, but the shock of the sekitori's answer saps his strength. The mountain spits blood onto the dohyō. And that is when the master drops his shinai. When he gives up his act of being an honorable teacher and reveals himself as another broken spirit. The old man launches his heavy fists into Akebono's jaw. And although the mountain is larger than anyone in the room, the boy lies there quietly as the sand of the dohyō becomes stained with blood.

The rikishi watch. They kneel on the floor in perfect posture until it is time to clean and sweep away the darkened sand in the ring, to carry their master to bed and the vessel of their former sekitori into the furnace.

COULD HARU HAVE REACTED WITH SUCH HONOR?

Could he have lain there as obediently as his sekitori, while his life was beaten out of his body? In the following weeks, the boy wonders this during every silence.

For the first time, Haru welcomes his routines, the training and chores, for the distraction they offer. Flashbacks to that night make him feel closer to the other rikishi, as if the trauma were some unseen glue binding them together.

Until one meal, when Haru stares down the black hole of a fellow wrestler's mouth—and he notices how swiftly the chopsticks of his training partner carry the meat and vegetables from their bowl, as if the wrestler's appetite had grown since the incident.

How can he eat this way?

Haru looks around the table in horror. He realizes the other rikishi are consuming the stew with similar ferocity, that he is the only one who struggles to eat. Revisiting his memory of that night, he recognizes that what he saw in their eyes had not been fear—but hunger. None of the wrestlers notice him doubling over; none of them notice him retching.

Eat with your knees facing the table, a voice lectures in his head. Haru imagines the smiling face of Akebono. *Don't you want to grow up strong, like me?*

Haru shakes his head. Will he ever be able to banish the sekitori from his memory? As his mind flashes to his oyakata raising the shinai, the boy realizes that he cannot unsee those atrocities nor forget his complicity. There is a part of him that does not wish to forget, but rather punish himself instead. Did Akebono not deserve at least that much?

In time, Haru abandons all desire he'd held of returning to his former life in the fields. He resigns himself to this fate. For if he cannot forgive himself, how can he expect a different reaction from his parents? Only years later, after Haru graduates into a sekitori, after he has wrestled the most powerful men in the most rarefied of arenas, clapping his hands to attract the attention of the Shinto gods before entering any ring—does he allow himself to revisit this period again. These weeks when he could have fled to the rice fields while the oyakata drank day and night in shame, when the other rikishi shirked their chores and paid him no attention, when he could have escaped.

It was easier for Haru to choose glory and the routines of sumo, to drink to oblivion every night, rather than to go home and hold the gentle gaze of his okāsan.

VISIONS PLAGUE HER MIND—OF HER SON FORGETTING, OF HIM tasting the chankonabe without expression, without recognition. Before the old woman arrives in Tokyo to attend the Grand Sumo Tournament, before she boards the back of her neighbor's truck, the mother confronts the inevitability that her chankonabe will turn cold. So, in her last pot of stew, the old woman forgoes the udon, accepting that the noodles could never survive the journey.

Along the way, strangers help. When the pot is too heavy. When young men and women at the train stations not only answer her questions—for the world has become a blur in her eyes and she cannot decipher the kanji on the map—but guide her onto the right platforms. Upon arriving in Tokyo, the woman remains reliant on the sons and daughters of others, those who gently accompany her through turnstiles and sometimes pay for her ticket. In another air-conditioned JR train, the old woman listens to the announcements carefully, grateful that the Yamanote Line travels in a circle so that even if she misses her stop, she will not be lost.

ELEVEN THOUSAND PEOPLE CROWD AROUND THE DOHYŌ IN Ryōgoku Kokugikan. Even the audience who paid for the farthest wooden benches sit shoulder to shoulder. The arena is filled with noise; it surpasses her grandest expectations from watching matches on television. The path to the ring is treacherous, a meandering line of steps beyond the limits of the woman's imagination, her unsteady gait, her vision.

The old woman's eyes overflow with grief. Her chankonabe will never get close enough to revive her boy's memories. How will she recognize her boy among the blur of wrestlers so far away? She knew him only as a child, before he joined the ranks of sumo.

The old woman drops her wooden cane, allowing it to clatter. Standing at the head of the steps, she summons all her energy to lift the pot—then yells her son's sumo name so loudly that even the referee turns toward her from the center of the ring.

Does it matter that every eye shifts in her direction before her fragile body crashes to the floor?

No, the old woman does not mind. For her final vision is that of a giant striding up the steps, trampling across the puddles of chankonabe, which ripple under his heart's weight.

SECOND MESSAGE

██████ at ██ : ██████

From an early age, I accepted that bravery was not one of my virtues.

Growing up in our Tower, I remember being terrified of the near daily thunderstorms during the monsoon season. Had we been able to afford living on a higher floor, my mother would surely have relocated us above the clouds, but raising me alone, she could not give us such luxuries. Instead, when the claps of thunder made my ears ring, she would drape a red blanket across my shoulders and hold me tightly in her arms. Then she would tell me to close my eyes, so as not to be blinded by the flashes of lightning.

I'll let you know when it's safe, she'd say.

Sometimes, when I opened my eyes in the hope that the worst had passed, I would catch my mother staring out at the storm through the floor-to-ceiling windows, smiling with a calm that I did not understand. It was as if she were admiring its destructive power. Then at the next strike of lightning, my head would drop again to her chest, my tiny hands too slow to cover my ears before the waves of thunder that followed.

There were moments when my mother's overprotectiveness irritated me, of course. Every time she yelled at me to wear slippers when I walked around with bare feet, I would roll my eyes. Upon reflection, she must have felt hurt every time I reacted to her care with derision, but my mother never stopped trying. It wasn't until I grew older that I realized how much she doted on me. For instance, although most of my education was conducted at home via Mindbank, my mother routinely knit me new robes so that my physical body would be more comfortable during the many hours I was connected to my lessons each day. Later, I was astounded to learn from my classmates that none of their parents had made clothes for them by hand.

As I recall these stories, I do not think I ever thanked her via voice for all the ways she took care of me during my childhood. Deep down, perhaps my mother always knew of my gratitude without my needing to express it.

Still, now that she's gone—how I wish that I could know for certain.

LATELY, AS I REFLECT ON MY INHERITANCE, I KEEP COMING BACK to the question of whether my mother truly meant for me to become a Dissident. Say a Qin citizen disregarded a law made by the Party—did that automatically make her an enemy of the state? Via my Mindbank, I had been taught that those two things were the same, but was that true?

The more I recall of my sheltered childhood, the more I think that my mother may have never meant to put me at risk by leaving me these memories. The mandate for Censors to review all inherited memories is relatively new; how many of us closely monitor updates to our empire's estate laws? Certainly, I did not know about the change until the memories arrived in my Mindbank along with a notice. Had my mother simply been unaware?

She must have known that her son was no hero.

Could she merely have wanted me to have these memories to remember her by, rather than turning them into objects of resistance? Perhaps she wanted me to taste the stew in *Chankonabe*, to understand the longing of the mother for her sumo-wrestler son as a reflection of her own love for me. Being unmarried, I wonder if the Memory Epic of the Regent's son and the American-white girl playing chess was meant to serve as a warning, for fear that I might fall in love with someone inappropriate like an immigrant from the Fourth World.

Not that any of this matters. It is too late now. The law is clear: the mere act of experiencing those memories, even if I did not share them with you on the Cloud, condemns me to be punished as a Dissident. It doesn't matter whether the law is fair, that I am young enough that the Gaokao was not such a distant experience, that I have yet to live a full life. It does not matter that if the Party asked, I would tell them that despite everything you witness in these memories, I remain thankful for the degree of safety and order in our society, along with my meaningful work improving the conditions of the Desert Colonies.

I am not one of those ungrateful citizens who fails to appreciate all the good that the Party has done for our people. Yet, my fate is sealed. It is a matter of time before my inheritance reaches the top of the Censors' work queue and the Red Guards arrive at my door.

For this reason, I do not deserve to be called a hero for sharing these memories. In my mother's stories, many of the protagonists too were unwillingly thrust into their moments of resistance. Often they pushed back, not out of moral clarity or courage but because the world had abandoned them, leaving them no choice but to rebel.

Tell me, if you were driven to the brink, wouldn't you feel compelled to resist too?

ONCE, AFTER A PARTICULARLY VIOLENT STORM, MY MOTHER gently touched my hand and told me that there had been a scientific breakthrough generations ago that would have made all Towers soundproof. By then, I had outgrown my childhood fears. But since the occasional thunderclap still triggered my migraines, I could not understand why our leaders would withhold such an innovation from their citizens.

It was the Party's choice not to implement it, she said.

Many moons later, I still recall the anger that flashed across her face when I pressed her, and the unfamiliar quiver in her voice when she answered.

They want to use nature to remind us to be afraid, my mother said bitterly as the red blanket we were sharing on the sofa slid to the floor.

It's their greatest source of power. Because they don't want us to know what it's like to live without fear.

AFTER THE BLOOM

Four hundred moons after the War, I gathered my things and fled home in the dead of night. Although I had repeatedly tried to explain why I needed to go, I was never able to make my mother or father understand. Unable to bear seeing the disappointment in their eyes that their only daughter could abandon them, and in desperate hope that a change of scenery might inspire me to finish my first novel, I mumbled my apologies to the wind.

Long before Mindbanks became available to the masses, I already worried that the written word was nearing its demise. Even prior to the buying and selling of memories, I'd witnessed bookstores in my neighborhood close, as fewer and fewer people read with the advent of social media and cinematic content produced by State-owned Enterprises. If Memory Epics were truly as immersive as the marketing claimed, I had little doubt that Mindbanks would soon become ubiquitous—then who would ever pick up a book again? I feared that if I did not soon write a truly exceptional novel, nobody in the world would ever know my name.

I had often felt as if there were a ticking clock in my head, running down the seconds toward irrelevance as an inner voice reminded me how unlikely I was to publish. When I moved away to a nameless town in Qin, to free myself from the distractions of home, I was surprised to find the voice only grew louder. For that reason, I wonder if I would have ever taken time away from my writing to meet Teacher Zhong, and discover his extraordinary collection of vintage watches, had the air conditioner in my rental not broken down that summer.

"It's sweltering in here!" Auntie Li said, fanning her face with a palm when she came to check on me after I moved into her studio. "I can see why you might not be comfortable." Frantically looking around my room for a distraction, my landlady began pointing at the old clock on the wall and telling me about the famous watch shop nearby.

"If you need a job, I believe Teacher Zhong is looking for an assistant. He is well respected for being the only watchmaker in the region and drawing wealthy visitors to our town. It would be a great honor to work for him," Auntie Li told me in a tone that suggested she was doing me a favor. As she spoke, I couldn't help but notice the beads of sweat glistening on her forehead, each one a tiny prism of sunlight from the window.

I wanted to tell Auntie Li that I already had a calling, and that she should respect writing as a profession, especially since I'd paid her two moons' rent up front to compensate for my lack of employment. Ever since I dropped out of college, my parents had pleaded for me to join them at the battery factory; had I wanted a job, I would've stayed home. For many moons before leaving school, I had dutifully scrimped and saved my graduate stipend, so I didn't need the money. Still, I knew better than to argue with my landlady. All I wanted was for the air conditioner to be fixed, so that I could write during the afternoons and sleep better at night; I was at her mercy. Pressing my lips, I gently asked if she might call her handyman soon.

"It may take a few days, I'm afraid. He is visiting his second family . . ." Her excuses trailed off when she noticed my face fall. "Do not worry, lovely girl. You can be patient for a week, yes? Please forgive this delay for your auntie."

My heart raced as I imagined losing another seven days of progress. Yet, just like with my parents, I recognized that there was nothing I could say to make her understand. Instead, I forced my expression into a smile befitting a pleasant, well-mannered girl. Even if all I wanted to do was scream.

I NEVER INTENDED TO VISIT TEACHER ZHONG'S SHOP THAT AFTER-noon. But to escape the heat, I soon abandoned my apartment. Crossing a nearby underpass to the town square, I began to explore the main shopping street. The watch store immediately caught my eye. Located close to a bronze monument of our Party founder, the shop looked nothing like the myriad stalls that surrounded it. Framed by a warm brick exterior, the glass display was filled not only with rows of old watches on plastic stands but also a line of chrysanthemums near its base. While most owners would have maximized the window space by showing more items for sale, I appreciated that the watchmaker had chosen to exhibit beauty instead.

The radiant flowers, coupled with the store's promise of air conditioning, beckoned to me. As soon as I walked through the doors, I became mesmerized by the splendor of the shop's dark wooden walls juxtaposed with the spotlights overhead. All around me were magnificent gold and steel watches, glimmering in their displays.

In time, I would study the history and scars of each precious piece in the shop, but on that first visit, I felt too overwhelmed to ask anything of the thin, stooped man at the back of the store. Bent over an opened wristwatch, its movement a mosaic of overlapping gears decorated with tiny red stones, the watchmaker had a gray magnifying loupe strapped to his head. Later, I would learn that specific wristwatch featured a stopwatch complication known as a chronograph, and that the insides had been hand-decorated with Côtes de Genève stripes. But on that day, all I noted was the calm that washed over me when Teacher Zhong welcomed me inside. Although he never glanced up from the table, nor let go of the sharp tools in his wizened hands, the warmth in his voice comforted me amid the unfamiliar opulence of his shop.

"Please. Make yourself feel at home. Let me know if you have any questions about the watches."

Sometimes, when I reflect on the past and imagine how my life would be different had I never met Teacher Zhong, I realize that I might never have learned what it means to love.

IN TRUTH, THE SHOP DID NOT NEED A FULL-TIME ASSISTANT. SINCE the watchmaker had been operating the store alone, part of me wondered whether he might have been charmed by my naivete and newfound horological interest. I had revealed in our first conversation that I was interested in working at his shop despite never having owned any serious watches. In the end, I decided that it must have been his desire to spend more time working on watches rather than managing clients that resulted in my hire.

From the beginning, I was surprised that Teacher Zhong never pressured me to make sales. "Do not rush. Take your time to study these pieces," he said. "Many of the watches are older than you or I. We should honor them by helping them find their right homes." I had never met a store owner like him before, at least not at any shop that sustained a profit.

Most afternoons we enjoyed a steady flow of customers, the quiet ticking of our store punctuated a few times an hour by the rush of an open door and the jangle of keys in a stranger's pocket. Despite the heat, the clients often arrived wearing dark suits—or red lab coats signaling their employment at the nearby research institute—and they were inevitably disappointed to find themselves sharing their needs with me rather than the great watchmaker they had traveled to consult. Nevertheless, whenever a client asked a question that I could not answer, I would go to the back of the store, where Teacher Zhong would be servicing watch movements on his desk.

I'd apologize for interrupting his concentration.

"No problem," the Teacher always said. While the clients' questions inexorably revolved around some minor issue—the originality of the signed crown, or if the lugs of the case showed any signs of polishing—I quickly learned that these small details meant everything to collectors. Before giving an answer, the watchmaker would rise from his seat and walk gingerly to the client, politely reaching forward with both hands to receive the watch before examining it using the loupe over his eye. Only then would he respond, pointing to relevant aspects of the watch. Not once did I see the Teacher express frustration at his clients, nor did he ever reprimand me for bringing him a question that I should have known how to answer.

"Look at the tiny digits below that star logo, on the gold Respirator," he once showed me after a client walked out in frustration due to my ignorance. "Do you see '28800' on that dial? It's no coincidence. That is how many times a four-hertz movement beats every hour, in contrast to the eighteen thousand beats of most vintage watches. All our timepieces run properly, but a higher frequency means that the watch will be more accurate, although the movement will suffer from more strain over time." He patiently waited for me to nod in understanding. "Seeing those numbers is the easiest way to determine whether a watch movement is a high beat when a customer asks; if you notice '28800' or '36000' printed on the dial."

He was generous with his knowledge, never making me feel foolish for how little I knew. When he agreed to hire me after learning of my admiration for the beauty in his store, I was initially nervous that he could be hiring me out of loneliness, to serve as his daily companion or entertainment. To my surprise, besides the occasional lectures on horology, he rarely engaged me in conversation. Sometimes we would go hours without speaking. Apart from watch inquiries, the other exception to his silences occurred whenever he overheard some uncouth client making an inappropriate advance toward me—then, the Teacher would snap out of his trance and yell from the back of the store, "Assistant, is someone bothering you?"

On occasion, he would get up from his desk specially to walk an offender to the door! At such moments, I was grateful that the old man cared more about my safety than any potential sale. In time, the term "Assistant" even took on an endearing quality.

"That is quite the story," Auntie Li exclaimed one evening as we sat in my studio. "When I suggested you meet Teacher Zhong, I never quite imagined him being such a protector. Everyone in town, we thought that all he cared about was his precious watches. We assumed that must have been what made him exceptional in his field." As she spoke, she peeled the skins off a half dozen clementines she'd brought from her apartment, dropping the rinds and fruit onto the paper towel between us on the bed. Leaning forward, she gestured for me to eat.

How could I disobey? I stuffed a clementine into my mouth, chewing on the fibrous core.

"Have you been able to write? While at work?" she asked.

I felt my face redden. Nodding, I admitted that when business was slow in the afternoons, I occasionally jotted down story ideas on my phone. When feeling inspired, I would outline chapters of the book.

"I'm sure that Teacher Zhong doesn't care, so long as you catalogue the stock list and take care of the customers," Auntie Li reassured me. "Speaking as another old person in this town, he probably appreciates your company. It's not easy being our age without children, watching the days pass so quickly."

I was too embarrassed to admit that I did not know exactly how old the Teacher was. Often I'd wondered whether the heavy curve of his back was a result of his poor posture rather than his age, but I never asked, for fear of offending him or drawing unwanted attention. Certainly I did not want him raising his head from his desk one day and wondering why my phone was always lit on the front counter.

"I think he lives on the second floor above the shop," I said abruptly, not sure why I was sharing this with Auntie. "Every evening when I lock up the store and pull down the metal grille, I notice the light above the shop turning on."

Auntie Li nodded.

"When I was your age, many men chased me. More than one asked me to be his wife," she said. "The reason I turned them down was that so many were obsessed with their work. It does not surprise me that Teacher Zhong is also like that." She shook her head. "But the truth is that you also worry me, you and your writing, because if you are not careful, you may turn into one of them too."

I opened my mouth, then shoved another piece of fruit inside. I appreciated that my landlady was looking out for me; I only wished she would also acknowledge the astonishing progress I had made on my book—more than three hundred pages over the last ten moons. As much as I tried to avoid thinking of my parents, I secretly hoped that Auntie Li could be proud of me in their place, rather than share their worries about my future.

"If you need a good husband recommendation, one of my friends manages several buildings in the province. She owns far more apartment units than I, and her lovely son—well, if you can look past his shyness, the boy's already got a Mindbank!"

She was still pointing at her right temple, where the memory drives were said to be surgically inserted, when I began to smile. Of course, most would have been impressed by her friend's apparent wealth. But as an aspiring writer, I still felt conflicted about how Memory Epics might one day eliminate my art form, the way that digital replaced film before the War.

Twice already Auntie Li had set me up with some boy from a nearby village. Sometimes I wondered whether that was why she brought so many fruits on her visits, so that my mouth would be too full to say no. Perhaps next time I could ask her to bring a plate of steamed sea bream, or another dish I enjoyed more.

Who knows what would have happened had the riots not ravaged our town a few weeks later? Perhaps my novel would now be complete, with critics praising the emotional resonance of the romance at its core. Perhaps I would have fallen in love with her friend's son over tea and introduced him to my parents. The truth is that nobody knows what would have happened had the Chrysanthemum Virus not come for us. Just like I will never know what might have materialized over the last hundred sheets of my manuscript.

In my mind, I can see those unwritten pages burning still.

I DO NOT BLAME ANYONE.

Had I paid more attention to the Party announcements that spring, routinely broadcasted from the loudspeakers on the main shopping street, maybe I could have guessed that something strange was about to happen. At the shop, we noticed that many of our regular out-of-town clients had stopped coming—whether to sell their watches or browse the new stock list—and we were forced to rely on our less affluent local customers to survive.

"Maybe the red lab coats from the research institute are getting a holiday," Teacher Zhong joked before promising that he'd continue to pay my salary even if business remained slow. I was too embarrassed by his kindness to ask how long he could afford to do that.

"It is a little odd," Auntie Li admitted one evening while dropping by with more fruits. I had asked her how everything was going, after noticing several empty units in her building. "Especially since the tenants who moved away—most of them had already paid their rent. They were some of my best. It wasn't like they didn't have the money to stay."

Standing at my door, Auntie rubbed her forehead anxiously. "Remember my friend with the shy son, the family with the Mindbanks? Anyway, I tried calling her this week—and her phone didn't even ring. She hasn't answered any of my messages."

I suggested that maybe the wireless outage announced by the Party last night was to blame. We had been warned that the State-owned Enterprise responsible for telecommunications in our province would require a week to repair the network.

"I messaged her before the outage but yes, that is strange too," Auntie Li said. "Seven days for repairs? I grew up in this town, and it never takes that long."

"Everything will be fine, Auntie." As I reassured her, I couldn't help but think about my parents, knowing how anxious they'd be in the same situation.

"The Party has never let us down," I said, repeating the line I had recited countless times during my university days, when I was still studying engineering to please others.

Auntie Li chuckled. "Sometimes, I forget that you are a college-educated woman. All that indoctrination in school, to have so much faith in our Leaders." I frowned, uncertain if my friend meant to sound sarcastic, but before I could react, she reached out and held both of my hands tightly. "Now you know why I never spent a fortune getting a Mindbank, for who knows who might be listening in on us?"

She grinned and placed the bag of remaining clementines in my hands. Then she walked toward the elevators. As I watched her silhouette shrink, I noticed she was wearing the same white dress she'd had on during one of our earliest encounters, when my air conditioner broke.

Would I look as beautiful, I wondered in envy, when I reached her age?

Such foolish thoughts. I regret little in my life, but that moment of vanity is among them.

Because the next time I would come across Auntie Li, her cheeks would be overcome with giant yellow flowers, her pale arms reaching toward the sky like the branches of an immortal tree—my dear friend leaning against an asphalt sidewalk, frozen in time and space.

IN TIME, THE SECRETS BEGAN TO REVEAL THEMSELVES, AS SURELY as the Chrysanthemum Virus infected its victims' faces. When the outbreaks spread from the research institute, the Party disconnected all telecommunication networks, and our military efficiently established perimeters around each infected town to prevent residents from leaving. Only the wealthiest citizens were secretly informed of the lab leak via Mindbank in the days preceding lockdown. It made me wonder whether my auntie would still be alive had she only trusted the Party. Of course, most of the rich fled without sharing the information with their neighbors, fearing that mass panic would make it more difficult to escape, so it is impossible to know if my friend would have warned me.

Sometimes it's easier not to know. Just as it was easier to look away upon seeing the yellow buds sprouting on the faces of the infected collapsed on the streets, the blooming flowers ripping through their skin before the paralysis and death set in. I tried not to dwell on the nightmare that the Virus may have reached my hometown as well; there was no way of knowing if my parents were still alive. Nor did we have any means of escape. When the young men dared to climb the freshly installed barbed-wire fences at the edge of town, we heard that the Qin soldiers on the other side did not hesitate to fire on them to enforce the quarantine. And when rumors spread that certain foods might ward off infection by the Virus, every supermarket and restaurant was looted overnight.

The violence was a natural progression of our desperation. By then, the rationale for the lockdown was clear: given how quickly the Chrysanthemum Virus killed the infected, the disease would soon burn itself out, as long as it did not find new hosts and mutate into a more resilient strain. The Party must have calculated that millions across the empire would perish if they attempted to treat the sick. It made sense to quarantine the affected towns instead, until any survivors would likely be resistant to the Virus, or even immune.

For the greater good of Qin.

Why should I resent the Party? It was mere coincidence that my town was among the hundreds of villages affected. Had I not disappointed my parents by dropping out of college, then fleeing home, perhaps I too would now be praising our Leaders for prioritizing the health of the nation over the deaths of an unlucky few.

IT IS DIFFICULT TO DESCRIBE WHAT I WITNESSED OVER THE NEXT two moons: the denial, then rage that swept across our town after we discovered that the Party had abandoned us, our collective emotions transforming into despair. Then came the first food riots, during which I largely huddled under the covers, trying to ignore the sirens outside. There was Auntie Li, then the little girl I saw writhing on the asphalt, face clustered with yellow flowers, screaming for somebody to save her.

None of that matters anymore. All you need to know is that in the chaos, as my food reserves dwindled, I started to hallucinate my parents' faces on the walls. In my loneliness, I even spoke to them. At first, I yelled at them for their lack of understanding, for pushing me away. Later, in moments of calm, I would apologize for not saying goodbye, for being too afraid of their anger in the weeks after I abandoned them to answer their messages. Now I was the one waiting for a response. But all I saw in my mind were their stern faces and disapproving eyes.

It was then that I realized that I did not want to die. Not yet, alone in that studio. Rising from my bed, I decided to say goodbye to Auntie's room for the last time, not bothering to lock up as I left.

Descending from the apartment, I stumbled toward the dark underpass to the town square, avoiding the bodies clustered with flowers
on the path. Emerging from the dark tunnel, I slowly made my way
to the main shopping street—where I knocked loudly on the grille
of Teacher Zhong's watch shop.

I called out his name.

Standing as straight as I could manage, I waited. Through the
walls of my apartment, I had heard the voices of families turning on
each other in the hallway; what could I possibly expect of my former
employer? By then, my hair had become so brittle that much of it
had fallen out; I had lost so much weight that my trousers barely
clung onto my waist. After avoiding the mirror in my bathroom for
the last moon, I could only imagine what I looked like now.

Nevertheless, I called out his name once more.

To my great surprise, the watchmaker appeared. Wearing a pink
gold watch on his wrist, he lifted the grille without a word to let me
into his ticking refuge. Inside, I collapsed onto the blue blanket that
he had laid out on the main floor beside the timepieces. By the time
the old man returned from upstairs with a bowl of five-grain rice, I
was fast asleep.

IT WAS FROM THE TEACHER THAT I LEARNED WHAT HAPPENED TO
the people who had tried climbing the barbed wire, and how the
wealthy had known to escape before the chrysanthemums began
appearing on our neighbors' bodies.

"I do not know for certain why neither of us has any symp-
toms," the watchmaker admitted during one of our conversations.
"Surely, over the past weeks, we've both crossed paths with the
infected. The only thing I can think of is that neither of us grew up
in this region. Maybe there's something in our genes or from our
childhoods that makes us immune."

I had assumed that the old man had been born in this town. I was embarrassed to realize that beside his love for timepieces, there was little I knew about him.

The Teacher chuckled when I asked about his upbringing.

"Oh, where should I begin?" he said. "I was born in Qin, but before the War, so it had a different name then. My father worked for the Party as an emissary to other nations. After my mother passed, we spent a few years living in the former capital of Qin-America, but my father quietly brought us back before the War." He tapped the scarred right side of his head. "For a brief time, I even had a prototype here!"

The privilege to own an early Mindbank? I struggled to imagine the old man as the son of some Party official. What happened to their wealth, their power? As I considered how I might ask without causing offense, the watchmaker seemed to anticipate my confusion.

"Given my father's position, it had been impossible not to make enemies during his career. After his retirement, they went after him on false charges of treason. We lost everything. It did not help that we adopted an American-white refugee."

"What?" I had never heard of such a tradition in Qin.

He nodded. "Her name was Jill. She was my best friend from the school I attended in Qin-America. She helped me survive in that place, taught me their culture, how to play chess." He laughed thinly. "Truth be told, many of my classmates' parents wore expensive watches, so that school was my first exposure to horology. Though I didn't realize it until later."

As we briefly locked eyes, I noticed the old man hesitate.

"Teacher Zhong, we don't have to keep talking about this. If you want to rest, I can keep watch while you sleep."

He shook his head. "No, all of this happened a long time ago, when I was still a boy. The War had just finished, and Qin citizens were beginning to recognize their higher status in the world, the changes in racial hierarchy." He swallowed deeply. "It's just hard sometimes to revisit that period and the path that led me here."

Spreading his arms, the man gestured toward the vast library of timepieces around us.

"I was young and in love. So I begged my father to petition the Party. She was living in an orphanage after the War, and I could not bear it." I heard the guilt in his voice. "My father's enemies may have come to destroy us regardless. But my actions gave them the perfect excuse."

The watchmaker stared at an empty spot on the floor.

"I loved her. Still, I understood from the beginning that she would resent me for what happened to her parents during the War. I accepted that she could never reciprocate my feelings, especially after I brought her to live with us in Qin."

Had he ever gifted her one of his watches? Perhaps a classic Calatrava, or a white Journe élégante if her wrist were larger.

"When my family lost everything, she left. Just packed up her things and disappeared," he said. "I try not to blame her. After the Party arrested my father, I wanted to restart my life elsewhere too. When I arrived in this town, the watchmaker who owned this store kindly took me in, accepted me as his new apprentice. Like you, I didn't have any experience."

I saw the sadness in the Teacher's eyes. As he spoke, I could not help but recall my unfinished manuscript. It too featured a forbidden relationship, between a quiet New Tianjin boy with a congenital heart defect and a girl from the northern hinterland of Hohhot. But it paled in comparison to the watchmaker's story.

I felt sick. The night I left home, I had promised myself that I wouldn't return until I had achieved a modicum of literary success, until I could place a copy of my novel before my parents, proving that their daughter had some worth. Yet, surrounded by all the clocks in that room, I realized that none of my tales could match the emotion in that old man's eyes, nor exceed the pain in his memories. The thought made me want to abandon my manuscript altogether.

I began to laugh out loud at my foolishness.

What was the likelihood that I would even survive the next few days, much less complete my novel? I struggled to imagine a world in which we came out of this nightmare alive.

"Sorry," the watchmaker said. "I know. All of this is so tragic that it's funny."

"Oh, no." I tried to explain that I was laughing at my own inadequacies, but before I could finish, he too broke out in hysterics.

We laughed together. We laughed at our despair until my intentions no longer mattered. We laughed until our bellies ached with more than hunger. Only then did I realize that we had no idea whether we had enough supplies to survive the lockdown. It was in that moment when I fully appreciated what the old man had done, the generosity he had demonstrated by letting me into the shop. He should have kept me out: I would have eventually fainted or gone away. By letting me in, he had placed his own survival at risk.

"Are you all right?" the old man asked. "All of a sudden you turned quiet."

Without warning, I embraced him with all the warmth that I could muster, wanting to show him the love that he always deserved, whether from that Qin-American girl or the Party that had wronged his family so long ago.

I held on tightly. For a long breath, I refused to let go.

DURING THE NEXT THREE MOONS WHEN QIN SOLDIERS WOULD examine and remove every flower-encrusted body from the streets, before they officially announced via loudspeaker that the quarantine would soon be over, Teacher Zhong would service every watch in the store. In his spare time, he taught me chess; by the end, my skills had progressed enough to make the watchmaker think for long periods during our games. When the Teacher tired of winning, he would ask me questions about my life. As our conversations grew more personal, we soon reached the topic of my novel, which of course, he had known about all along from Auntie Li.

"I'm happy that you were able to stay productive when we didn't have customers," he said graciously. "Now, you can entertain me by telling me what happens in your book."

Embarrassed, I told him that there was nothing special about my novel. "It's a simple romance between a New Tianjin boy and a girl from Hohhot. The chapters alternate between their perspectives." When he insisted that I say more about the plot, I realized that I had never described my book to anyone before. "Sorry, I'm not used to this. Anyway, these days with Mindbanks, I doubt anyone will care about what I write . . ."

"I care."

A lump formed in my throat; I turned away. Composing myself, I began to share some of my favorite scenes in the book—the first time that they lock eyes in the decorative fan factory owned by the boy's family, where the girl makes her living as a migrant worker; their impulse trip to Inner Mongolia to meet her parents, rightfully worried that no Tianjin family would allow their son to marry someone from "the countryside," even if Hohhot was the capital of its province.

"The girl's father has a heart-shaped mole on his face, just like the one my father carries on his right cheek." I started to tell the Teacher about the sacrifices my parents had made for me: For as long as I could remember, they had worked fourteen-hour days at the battery-manufacturing plant, all so that their daughter could be the first in their family to attend college. I admitted that even in my angriest moments, I understood that their lack of support for my writing came out of fear rather than malice, that they were terrified I would not be able to support myself after they were gone. Just because their worries were distressingly stereotypical did not make them invalid. I appreciated that they wanted to save me the disappointment of having my heart broken if nobody recognized the quality of my work, even if I wanted the freedom to choose whether to take the risk myself.

As I talked about my parents, I realized how many of my characters had been written in their image. "My father's favorite dish is wu-chang sea bream, just like the Hohhot girl's," I revealed. "I meant to change it, but never got around to it."

The Teacher smiled. "When was the last time you talked to them?"

I did not want to answer, unable to bear the disappointment on my mentor's face once he learned that I had not spoken to my parents for more than a dozen moons. I wondered whether I'd be able to distract him by asking about one of the alarm watches in the room, such as the blue Memovox or oversized Cricket in the corner. But before I could open my mouth, our phones began buzzing in a symphony of pings as the Party reconnected our telecommunications grid.

"Wait, one minute. I'm receiving messages . . ."

I gasped. The first words to arrive on my phone were from my mother. And as I read every frenzied text from her, asking whether I was in one of the infected towns or begging me to come home, I could not stop the tears from streaming down my face. It felt impossible to reconcile my relief that my parents still cared about me with the shame of having abandoned them. And the newfound hope that I might see them again.

"Take your time," the Teacher said gently before I leaned over to show him the flood of messages. "What matters more than these moments, right?"

I briefly thought of the night I fled home, then shook my head with shame.

WE PASSED THROUGH MANY QUARANTINE CENTERS ON THE journey back to my hometown.

Every time we survivors reached a checkpoint, a new Party

official would request that we be reexamined by another squadron of masked medical professionals. We understood their caution, but it was frustrating to be treated like pariahs after having endured so much. When another nurse punctured me with a needle, I would think of Auntie Li and pray that I had not imagined the final expression of peace on her face, beneath the yellow flowers occluding her features. While waiting for my blood results, I would admire the extraordinary gift Teacher Zhong had given me the day we parted.

"So you won't forget this old fool," he said, placing the watch on my wrist. The rose-gold case rested on my arm perfectly. How had he known that I'd always preferred that metal to the more ostentatious nature of yellow gold or the weight of platinum? It was the same watch he had worn while offering me refuge several moons ago. Besides being a perpetual calendar, it featured a chronograph function, along with a moon phase subdial.

It was worth a small fortune.

I was breathless as I thanked him. Even as I tried to say that his gift was too valuable for me to accept, I couldn't bring myself to remove the magnificent timepiece from my wrist.

The old man scoffed. "It's rude to decline a present from your elder."

He revealed that the calendar had originally been a gift from the Patek brand to his father. "These moons with you remind me that I can form new memories, happier ones. I don't need mementos of the people I lost," he said. "Seeing it on your wrist now brings me joy. Just promise me that you'll honor it by wearing it. And if the opportunity presents itself, pass it down."

Perhaps if we'd had more time, I would've found the will to return that beautiful watch to him. But on that afternoon, we were not alone. Three soldiers swathed in personal protective equipment stood by the shop door. Despite their politeness, I could tell that they were impatient men who wouldn't hesitate to grab my elbow and lead me out to one of the marked trucks. I didn't want to cause the soldiers any trouble, not when they would soon accompany me on the caravan of other survivors traveling across Qin to reunite with our families.

In the end, I convinced myself that I could give back the perpetual calendar to Teacher Zhong later, that I would merely serve as its guardian until I saw him again. When I waved goodbye to my friend, my mind was so preoccupied with the beauty of his unexpected gift that I failed to even register a final glimpse of his tender face. Of course I couldn't have predicted that my journey home would take more than three moons. Or that the Teacher would fall gravely ill while I was in transit.

I remain thankful that in his last weeks, the soldiers allowed me to call him often on my phone. We would joke around, reminiscing about our favorite clients from the store. His was an elderly scientist whose eyes would bulge out of her glasses upon seeing any hint of tropical patina on a dial. Mine was a skinny man who adored vintage Cartier; he would make the most nonsensical jokes but laugh at them with such fervor that we would end up joining him anyway.

"Are you wearing it?" the Teacher would ask abruptly, more as his memory worsened. Gazing at my wrist, I'd reassure him that I was taking good care of his gift. I promised him that I would never sell the watch. That if I had children, one of them would act as its next steward.

"Speaking of another generation, have you talked to your mother and father today?"

Most days, I answered honestly. Other times, I lied to make him happy, the way I wish I had with my parents.

BY THE TIME YOU READ THIS JOURNAL, I DO NOT KNOW WHERE I will be.

Perhaps my novel will be finished, transformed from the premise I described in the vintage watch shop. Or maybe it will remain incomplete forever. Perhaps these very reflections of my time with the watchmaker have been adapted, and you are reliving them as entertainment via your Mindbanks, which have become increasingly popular of late.

I don't mind. Now that the Teacher can no longer receive my calls, I am content to spend the rest of my journey on the caravan staring at the meandering roads ahead. When the nausea becomes too much, I close my eyes in search of calm; often I find myself comforted by the strange phantasmagoria of scenes forming in my mind.

Among the recurring scenes, I'll share the one that repeats the most. There in my imagination, I stand beyond the gates of a gray quarantine center, which did not exist when I left but I somehow know is in my hometown—and for the first time in eighteen moons, I see my father and mother in the distance. As with the building, my mind cannot perfectly reproduce my parents' faces, but I recognize them anyway. In the next instant, my father appears in front of me. He wraps his skinny arms around my waist, his grizzled beard scraping my cheek and making me recall the father from Hohhot I once described on a page. Before I can speak, my mother hugs us both, so tightly that she nearly drops the hot container of steamed fish she made to welcome me back into their lives.

They simultaneously ask me about my book, which is how I know this is nothing more than a fantasy. Then in that moment, I glance at the rose gold watch on my wrist and think of the Teacher, who cared for me no matter if my talent was worthy of his love and grace.

SWIMMER OF YANGTZE

The boy had been born with four healthy limbs, but by the end of his first year he had already lost both his arms. Broad, toned shoulders even in childhood gave him the triangular physique that so many young men craved, as if his upper body were perfectly fitted for a Zhongshan tunic suit—although if he were to have worn one, his father would have needed to trim the sleeves off so as to draw less attention to his son's missing limbs beneath the blue and black cloth.

Both his parents worked as tailors in our humble village near Wuhan, as their own forefathers had done. They had been born during the glorious years of the Long March and the rise of our Communist Party; recently they had enjoyed the fortune of watching our leader, Chairman Mao, dive into the Yangtze River to swim against "the great wind and great waves of the bourgeois." Oh, how lucky we all had been to witness the launch of our Cultural Revolution! Only two days after the swim, Chairman Mao—may he live for ten thousand years!—returned to the Great Hall of the People in Beijing to arrest that traitor Liu Shaoqi, who died a mere three years later after a too-few number of public beatings at Party denunciation meetings.

As a baby, the Swimmer had been ordinary. He cried, as all boys do while they get used to empty stomachs. He was skinny but not overly malnourished. Almost daily he had been breastfed by his mother, until she fell sick from some evil curse that the doctor had called pneumonia and would later sour her milk. For the next year, his father would stitch an extra Zhongshan suit each week to afford the extra cost of cow milk for his only son.

Soon the rumor would spread all over the village near Wuhan that the Swimmer's mother could no longer give birth; for why else would the tailor not have compelled his wife to try again for another child, one not so accursed?

Still, the story of how the boy lost his arms remains a mystery. Some whispered that it was caused by some fungus stemming from the baby's long baths in the Yangtze, since the tailor's shop near the river had also served as their family sleeping quarters. Others say his disease was genetic, but to those gossipers, I ask: why did his ailment affect only his arms and not the rest of his body? All we know for certain is that when the boy was barely eight months old—and he is truly blessed by the Holy Buddha that he was too young to remember this—his parents took him to Wuhan Children's Hospital one evening and when they returned, their child no longer had arms. Later, the rumor flooded our village that the father had locked himself inside his workshop for three straight days after returning from the hospital: all so that he could sew a new set of clothes for his boy, none of which bore a single sleeve.

His mother must have been devastated! First, her son had lost his arms. But then her pneumonia began to give her such severe headaches that she could no longer help her husband with his tailor shop; and of course this only tightened money matters more.

What to do with a boy with no arms? Sure, he did not need to flip over the pages of old texts written by such patriotic poets as Li Bai or Du Fu, but also he did not have any hands to feel the fine wrinkles in a piece of fabric or operate a sewing machine. Who would inherit his family's shop?

Many in the village wondered about this. For many years, as the boy grew into his body, they would gossip over bowls of noodles, making bets about when the tailor might sell his shop on the cheap. I, of course, did none of this and flashed evil eyes when I heard them whisper about the tailor and his armless son; until news spread to my door one night that the tailor's wife, bedridden once more, had breathed her last. And then not even I had any choice but to ponder such business matters.

ONE MORNING, A FEW FROM OUR VILLAGE SAW HIS LITTLE BODY in the Yangtze, thrashing against the current while kicking like a river dolphin in the water.

And we had thought every baiji in the Yangtze had already passed away!

The sky was clear that day, I hear, although this did not matter, given the Yangtze's murky nature. The first time that I saw him practice, I was rushing from the market to see his father about a tear in my wife's blouse when, suddenly, I noticed the armless boy surging across the river. Lying on his back, his small body undulated as if he were a wave himself. At each crest, he lifted his head to take in new gulps of air—as if gasping for life—before sinking back beneath the water.

I feared that the boy was drowning! But as I watched him, I soon became transfixed by the smoothness of his rhythmic motion, his body moving effortlessly through the river like a long muscle. Perhaps it was only the sun playing tricks with these old eyes, but in the bubbles formed by the water his body displaced I began to imagine sinewy arms extending from his shoulders.

So graceful and natural were the movements of his body in the Yangtze.

A deep and grating voice cut across my thoughts.

"Tell me, old man: that boy in the river—he is not one of this village, is he?" I turned to see a stranger standing in front of an easel, leaning slightly toward the river as he painted the First Wuhan Yangtze Bridge. He spread dabbles of color upon white paper as he continued his musing. "He swims as if he belongs to the water itself."

What rudeness from this man to interrupt my silence! And he was not even from our village. "Yes, he is the son of my tailor—and he has no arms," I said. "You would do better to paint him instead."

"Really, is that right?" the visitor said. He stared at the Swimmer floating in the river. "He must have strong legs."

Yes—all of this was true. But later, when I spoke with the tailor at his shop, he boasted that his son's most impressive feature was not his legs, but rather his feet. It was their extraordinary dexterity that allowed the boy to brush his teeth with his toes and even pick up chopsticks to enjoy his favorite dish of steamed wu-chang fish—or so the tailor told me.

"Why does he swim every day without fail?" I asked the boy's father. "Does he never tire? I hear that he sometimes enters the water in the morning—and when sunset arrives, he is still one with the river." The tailor replied that he did not know. Yet later, when the newspapers began to write about his son, he suddenly became confident of the reason.

"For the Communist government and our great Chairman Mao Zedong!" Those words were quoted in his name and printed in the *Chang Jiang Daily Press* under the headline "Boy with No Arms Swims Across Yangtze." Soon, reporters from other cities in the province of Hubei were traveling to Wuhan too to write about the Swimmer; and one day, I even heard that a famous reporter from Xinhua Beijing had arrived at our train station.

So much attention bestowed upon our humble village! Not since the grace of our Chairman's swim in the Yangtze had we enjoyed such attention. From morning to dusk, reporters would crowd along the edge of the river to take photographs of the Swimmer practicing his dolphin kicks in the cloudy water. At the beginning of this commotion, a few local boys—no doubt among them the no-good sons of Four-Eyes Ah-Fong and Shiny-Head Lao Cheng—followed the Swimmer into the river in hopes of being photographed too. But barely one week passed before those local boys gave up their foolish ambitions, as stories of the armless swimmer continued to be printed in every paper while their own faces remained unseen.

Soon, the tailor's son returned to being the only Swimmer in the Yangtze.

"You are so lucky!" every villager in Wuhan told the father. And indeed, before long, he became known as the most famous tailor in all of Hubei.

Sometimes he would even turn away business. "My son is the Swimmer of Yangtze," the tailor would explain if he felt too tired to work. And because of his child's reputation, nobody he rejected was ever upset.

One morning, I was eating a bowl of la-mian at Four-Eyed Ah-Fong's noodle stand when a group of villagers appeared at our table to share news that the Swimmer had gone missing. Immediately I dropped the chopsticks from my hand and rose from my wooden stool to look for Ah-Fong to tell him that I would return to finish my food later—but already, that no-good noodle-stall operator had gone to the river to see with his own eyes.

And behold: in the Yangtze, there was no Swimmer!

"What has befallen the Swimmer of Yangtze?" everyone cried, circling the riverbank. More quietly, they asked: how would this affect business? For months, our stalls had been surging with profits because of tourists traveling from all over our country to see the Swimmer, and now we were afraid, for many of us had expanded our shops to accommodate this traffic.

"All is well!" a voice called out. From the riverbank, the familiar shape of the tailor began walking toward our panicked crowd.

"Where is your son? Is he ill?" Four-Eyed Ah-Fong asked.

"Has he been kidnapped by some enemy of our village? Will he be back swimming soon?" Shiny-Head Lao Cheng followed.

A rumbling laugh exploded from the tailor, a sound I had never heard before in my many years visiting his shop. "My son, the Swimmer of Yangtze, is healthy and well. But he is not in Wuhan anymore—because the great Communist Party, led by our leader Chairman Mao, has summoned him to Beijing to swim for our People's Republic!"

At first, I was too shocked to speak. Would our great Communist Party, twenty years after its heroic liberation of our country, truly call upon this boy to represent them? Even if that were true, would they disappear him from our village overnight? Not possible!

But then, as the tailor began to explain how Red Army comrades had arrived last night at his shop bearing important documents from Beijing, we suddenly noticed the brown piece of paper he held between his fingers. And after Four-Eyed Ah-Fong snatched the letter from the tailor's soft hands, that no-good noodle-stall operator unfurled it in the air for all of us to see—and indeed there upon the page was the signature of our Chairman Mao himself!

Oh, what glorious pride I felt! "Will he be swimming for the international games?" I asked.

"Yes!" the tailor said. His son would race in the competition for swimmers with disabilities, which also happened every four years, and that news made us no less proud.

By the river that day, we showered the tailor with congratulations. And the next morning, when I brought over some meat and rice rations for the tailor, I saw a mountain of gifts piled up on the ground outside his shop, like an offering to the Holy Buddha himself.

"Home of the Great Swimmer of Yangtze" the tailor had stitched onto a long piece of fabric, which he fastened onto his front door. Soon, even the mayor of Wuhan traveled down to the riverbank to meet the tailor and commission him to sew those same words upon a banner to be strung between the twin red pillars of the city's dragon gate—so that all who walked underneath would know our village's great honor.

Three nights later when the mayor hoisted the banner high between the twin dragons, all of Wuhan erupted with the sound of firecrackers.

IN THE SUMMER OF 1976, WITH BUSINESS BOOMING IN OUR VIL-lage beside Wuhan, Shiny-Head Lao Cheng bought the first television in town. He had timed this purchase perfectly, so that he could show off his electric box during the international games he knew we all wanted to watch.

"As a village, we will witness our great hero win—the Swimmer of Yangtze!" he shouted, pointing at his small television. He had set it up outside his house in the town square near the red dragon gate and we cheered his generosity, as if the selfless spirit of the model comrade Lei Feng had been reborn.

On the evening of the swim, even the tailor came from the river-bank to watch. Shiny-Head Lao Cheng offered him the best seat, in front of the television, while the rest of us crowded around, elbowing one another for a better view of the black-and-white screen. Then, after too many hours of watching other competitions—for apparently those without limbs competed at many sports—we finally saw our hero in the pool. He was the only Chinese athlete. In the water, our Swimmer jumped up and down, nodding vigorously at the crowd of foreigners; for of course, he had no arms with which to wave and earn their cheers.

But in our village, and almost certainly all of Wuhan, we were shouting for only one Swimmer, and that was the Swimmer of Yangtze!

As the race was about to start, our hero placed both his feet against the wall and turned his back toward the other end of the pool. Ah, so he would be swimming backstroke. Pressed up to near-standing while facing the wall, the Swimmer held himself frozen in the air, clenching between his teeth a white towel held out by his coach, who knelt upon the deck and stared into the boy's eyes.

Go, Swimmer of Yangtze! I was so nervous that my arthritic hands began to cramp.

We heard the gunshot—and the Swimmer was pulsing through the water!

"Add oil, Swimmer of Yangtze!" we cheered. There on the flickering black-and-white screen were the same dolphin kicks we had seen him practice in the Yangtze, triumphing over its heavy current. At the end of the wall, we saw him flip underwater and begin those kicks again.

So what if most of his foreign competitors had one or even two working arms? They were cheaters! They used their legs as if they were swimming freestyle with single-arm strokes, but none of them could gain a lead while the Swimmer kicked like a dolphin.

Then, as we heard the cheers grow louder from the electric box—and oh, how marvelous was that foreign invention—we realized that the race was nearing its closing stretch, and still the Swimmer of Yangtze was ahead!

"Add oil, our young hero!" we cried again. But soon we saw that our hero was starting to grow tired and slow—he was ahead now by no more than one half stroke. And when the three fastest swimmers turned to swim the final lap, the two foreigners behind our hero began to extend their limbs, and so the Swimmer of Yangtze—and this I would not have believed without seeing it with my own eyes—surged past both their outstretched arms by kicking full-speed until he rammed his head straight into the concrete wall!

Our village fell silent. We watched as a shiver shot through his body like an electric shock, before he went limp and dropped beneath the surface of the water. The Chinese coach, who had held out the towel for the Swimmer at the beginning of the race, dove into the pool.

Then, a voice rang out from the electric box and we learned our dreams had come true—the Swimmer of Yangtze had won!

All of us sitting down leapt from our chairs in joy, while those standing jumped even higher. Some of us were crying, tears streaming down our faces. A gold medal for China! Because of our brave hero from the village!

Everyone except for the Swimmer's father, of course, who had wanted to hear news of his son's health. All of us assured him that his son would be fine.

"He is a hero, so young and strong," we said, "Our Holy Buddha would never allow any harm to come to him." And soon enough, the electric box would pan out to show the armless boy lifting his head from the pool deck to smile at the camera, with little more than a bloody wound on his head, and every one of us shouted in the tailor's ear, "See! Your son is fine!"

Later, the Swimmer of Yangtze would stand on the highest podium step, between the two foreigners who had finished behind him. A white man in a black suit—and we could tell from just watching the electric box that his garment's fabric was finer than any the tailor could have fashioned—walked over to the podium to hang a moon-shaped medal over our hero's neck. In his other hand, the white man held out a bouquet of flowers; for a moment, the Swimmer seemed to pause and circle the pool with blinking eyes. Then he wordlessly took the bouquet into his mouth, clenching the stems of each young flower with his teeth, and folded over in a deep bow.

Oh, how every heart in our village exploded in that moment with pride!

A FEW MONTHS LATER, WHEN THE SWIMMER ARRIVED HOME AT the Wuhan train station, a group of us gathered outside in welcome. Around his neck, he wore the same medal we had admired on the electric box; except in real life, we saw how the metal shone underneath the sun and we whispered that it must have been made of real gold. That night, the mayor announced a spectacular ceremony in the town square, to celebrate the Swimmer's return.

But it is true that even then, we could see that the boy's head was not quite right. During the ceremony, he smiled a few times at us in the crowd, but his eyes were glazed over and he would often shake his head from side to side without reason. Later, when I asked his father when his son might return to Beijing, the tailor pretended not to have heard me and walked away.

Such audacity and disrespect—to his elder, no less! Worse yet, as that man was leaving, he was muttering underneath his breath; and if only he had been facing my better ear, I would have heard each word and then known how to scold him the best way.

In the end, we never did see the boy float again in the Yangtze— although a crowd did gather by the river for many days after the ceremony in hopes of watching his triumphant return to the water, a glorious event that never happened.

So this is the story of how the Swimmer of Yangtze stopped entering the water and became ordinary once more. For a long time afterward, the townsfolk still brought their business to the tailor, so that they could touch that gold medal his son wore around his neck. But then one night, a group of thieves broke into the tailor's house and stole that boy's treasure while he lay asleep. And the next morning, when the tailor awoke, he saw that the thieves had also cut down that famous fabric, which had hung above his door: the one that had read "Home of the Great Swimmer of Yangtze."

Over time, most of our village stopped going to that tailor shop, for we had heard a rumor that the Yangtze was polluted and it would be bad for our children to breathe in the chemicals rising from the river. Still, once in a while, I would travel to that riverbank to bring the tailor a torn jacket or duvet from my wife. Sometimes on those visits, I would glimpse that armless boy sitting on the ground of his father's shop, often not even wearing a white shirt upon his back as he folded clothes with his toes. But whenever my eyes wandered to meet his, the boy would kick up to his feet with the same force I had once witnessed in the Yangtze River, and then run off. And so, I was never able to exchange words with him—to ask why he never swam again for our Party, or uncover any other mysteries, for that matter.

Recently though, I noticed that the wooden planks holding up the tailor shop were beginning to crack. Sitting inside, I suggested to the tailor that he see Shiny-Head Lao Cheng to bargain for some cheap repairs. For a while, I waited to hear his gratitude. But when the words I expected did not arrive, I repeated my advice loudly.

"Do this," I said, "before the river flood comes to wash your shop away."

Still, that man did not answer! My old hands tightened.

"Have you lost your ears, tailor! Do you want to die?"

A long pause followed my words. The tailor tilted his head.

"If my son and I were to drown in the Yangtze," he said slowly, "would such tragedy not serve our village, to make its name more glorious?"

How shocked I was to hear this blasphemy come from his mouth! Not only my hands, but now my arms were shaking too as I stood, ready to shout foul curses at the tailor's head.

But then just as my lips began to part, I saw that boy with no arms, sitting in the dirt. Hunched over, he abruptly lifted his chest to reveal his bare shoulders hemmed in by empty space. Our eyes met and he paused his rising motion. Only this time, the boy did not run or swim away but instead twisted his head upward, gasping for air.

INNOCENTS

The Elder assigned to our Tower was a retired historian, a faithful servant of the Party. The tenant before him had been sent away for reeducation, so the reward of the empty apartment had not cost the Party any coin. Still, had my son not run amok, banging on the door of every neighbor on our floor, it is possible that none of us in the Tower would have realized that the Elder had already moved in.

It was not Ren's first time getting into such mischief; as a result, none of our neighbors had bothered to answer, save for the old man. Upon seeing my boy, the Elder broke into a radiant smile and invited him into his home. Or so my son described afterward to me in excitement.

"Mama, he wears a gray beard!"

Ren was jumping up and down, reminding me of the langur monkeys I knew he had seen in a Memory Epic featuring zoos. He tried to send me a memory of the conversation via Mindbank so that I might appreciate the old man's appearance, but Ren's enthusiasm only made me more anxious about the newcomer on our floor. Noting the fatigue on my boy's face, I suggested gently that he retire to his room instead.

My son protested, of course. But he obeyed in the end, his tiny feet sliding across the floor as quiet as a shadow.

SUCH HAD BEEN THE EXTENT OF MY BOY'S PUNISHMENT, I INformed the Elder meekly. As I stood before his door the next day, I reminded myself to keep my head bowed out of respect.

To my surprise, from the corner of my eye, I saw the old man nod approvingly.

"It is good that you did not hit him." He stroked his beard. The man was shorter than the reincarnation of Confucius my mind had conjured from my son's description. "We are neighbors now. Please drop the formalities," he said. "There is no need to call me Elder Han every time."

Slowly, I raised my head, even as I knew that I could never acquiesce to the historian's request for informality. Befitting his seniority, the Elder wore long gray robes that matched the sea of wrinkles on his face. His hair was knotted at the top of his head in the scholarly fashion that had become popular in recent moons, an ode to our glorious Qin past. As the man smiled, his eyes darted down the hallway, as if expecting someone to be watching us.

"You remind me of someone from my youth, Ms. Wu." Sweeping an arm behind him, the Elder invited me to enter. "I was just about to brew a fresh pot of dragonwell tea."

I remained silent and peered into the living room. The morning sun cast a series of misshapen silhouettes of furniture onto the hardwood floor; I closed my eyes, trying to shake off every memory of the afternoons I had spent inside. I refused the old man twice but eventually accepted, as if anyone could deny an Elder three times.

"Forgive the clutter," he said in a perfunctory manner. He pointed at the long, white dining table with legs that I knew would wobble if we did not weigh down the surface. A cane leaned against the table at the end of the room, surrounded by eight lavishly carved banyan chairs. Next to the table was a large marble counter that the previous tenant had added six moons ago to separate the dining area from the kitchen. "I would have tidied in advance had I known that a guest might grace my home." Contrary to the modesty in his words, I could tell that the living room had been dusted. Still, the Elder had not made any significant renovations. He must have arrived in the apartment less than a week ago.

"Most of this furniture belonged to the old tenant. I apologize for his taste. You must understand that at my age, I did not feel up to the task of redecorating so soon after moving," the Elder said. "As if I would ever buy such a large table! Why would anyone need to host so many guests in one place? And in the flesh?"

His laughter reverberated around the walls until the sound began to die in his throat.

The room fell silent as I assessed his reaction. Had he remembered that the old tenant was not a stranger to me, but my neighbor? As I watched him stroke his beard, I wondered whether the Party had informed him of my family's loyalty.

I waited briefly, then cleared my throat.

"The man who lived here before did not behave honorably," I started, allowing my voice to tremble with the gravity of my neighbor's sins. "Clearly, I did not know him. Perhaps none in our Tower truly did. We were all in the dark with regards to his betrayal."

As the Elder relaxed, I gave myself permission to release my breath. If only it were that easy to resolve the tensions in our Tower. Ever since the Red Guards conducted the eviction last moon, most of our neighbors had been on tenterhooks, turning into recluses for fear that they might be the next to be reported for disloyalty to our government. It almost did not matter what the charges were. Any hint of suspicion resulting from a neighbor's report was enough to vanish an entire family. Already there was talk of our trash being monitored by patriotic volunteers.

Had the Elder ever visited a reeducation camp before? An image of handcuffs shackled to a metal bed frame flashed across my mind, although I had never witnessed such punishments myself. Of all people, he might know the truth behind the rumors of those men and women who had been "disappeared."

For a second, I imagined cold steel wrapped around Ren's thin wrists.

"Yes, yes," the Elder said. "Nobody could blame your family for your neighbor's betrayal. My only hope is that the Dissident receives the treatment he needs. Such a tragedy. Perhaps one day he may repair some of the damage he caused."

What damage? I wanted to ask. *And to whom?* I bowed again, to hide my confusion.

"It was welcome news to hear that a former historian would be joining our Tower," I said softly, wondering if flattery might loosen the old man's lips. "We need your leadership, especially now."

Perhaps I should have told him the whole truth then. It would have adequately demonstrated evidence of my fealty. But if there was one rumor that I did not want to spread, it was our family's special relationship to the Party. Besides our neighbors' scorn, there was the risk of retribution, especially if the Dissident had allies remaining in the Tower.

I shivered.

Sensing my unease, the Elder pulled out one of the banyan chairs and gestured for me to sit. The impulse of this old man to take care of me, rather than the other way around, made me blush. For an instant, I was tempted to tell him the truth about my son; then I realized that his unexpected kindness could be a tactic to make me lower my guard.

"Apologies, I have gotten so used to living alone that I have forgotten my manners," he said. "Did you still want some tea?"

The Elder settled into his chair, knowing that I would not inconvenience him now. Then, as my eyes looked beyond his head to the rest of the room, I gasped—for hanging on the back wall was a large decorative fan made of beechwood panels, featuring a red-crowned crane.

How had I missed it? There had not been a painting in the apartment before. The tall bird returned my stare with one of its thin legs raised accusingly, its piercing eyes seeming to follow me across the room. Only twice via Mindbank had I seen such a creature. Yet I had not appreciated their noble bearings before, or their vibrant colors.

"Ah, I was wondering when you might notice. Such paintings cannot rival the portraits of our Party leaders, but it is still a fine piece of art, a reward from the Criminal Archives for my service . . . Did you know that Qin emperors once trained these birds to dance to guqin music?"

I apologized for my unseemly reaction. First the boy, then myself, I said. How will my family ever atone for our behavior?

My words made the Elder laugh harder. "When will you stop apologizing, Ms. Wu!"

I lowered my head. His friendliness did little to assuage my fears, although I felt relief that he did not appear to be the kind of vile man who would use his esteemed status to extort women for sexual favors. Surely the Party had told him about what I had done to prove my loyalty before inviting him to our floor? But what if the Dissident had fed them lies under interrogation? Every visit I made to this apartment could have been spitefully reframed by the Dissident to suggest that my family had been accomplices in his movement.

Had this old man been sent here to investigate such accusations? It would take only one slip to ruin us. Whether or not we were faithful servants, the Party would take no risks.

"Perhaps if I can bring one issue to your attention," the Elder murmured. "When your son came to my door yesterday, out of curiosity I asked the boy what memories had been uploaded recently to his Mindbank . . ."

I cursed in my head. What secrets had Ren unwittingly revealed? I regretted using my son as an excuse to meet the Elder; I wished that I could have taken advantage of that custom from former Qin-America, where it had apparently not been unusual for neighbors to bake cakes and then knock on the doors of new tenants to welcome them to the building.

"Forgive me," the Elder continued, "I could not help noticing that everything in his Mindbank was related to science—and nothing of our Party's glorious history!"

I sat in confused silence.

"Of course, I do not intend to critique your parenting, or what memories you acquired for your son's education," the Elder added. He had already checked and discovered that Ren was following one of the recommended curricula; nevertheless, it frustrated the historian that each ensuing generation seemed to be growing more ignorant.

"It's almost as if young people don't believe in the relevance of history anymore!" The old man slammed his wrinkled palm on the table with surprising force. "Given Mindbanks, you'd think we would have already achieved the perfect preservation of our past via memory records, but no—quite the opposite!"

What was he trying to insinuate? Whenever the Party mandated that we delete any newly illicit Memory Epics, such as the Dissident romance *I Had Too Much to Dream*, I had always removed them before the deadline, even when I could have hidden them on a private drive in my Mindbank.

"What do you think, Ms. Wu?" The Elder turned his gaze in my direction.

I did not answer, hoping that the question would just go away. I had long learned the benefit of allowing men to treat me as if I were a piece of furniture; quietly, I weighed which of my views might be safe to share. How would this man react if he knew that Ren had been born with a Chrysanthemum Mutation? Would he still speak to me with respect?

Not wanting to risk offense, I thanked him for his views.

"No, you're not getting out of the question so easily, Ms. Wu," he said. "It's not as if I'm asking you to download any illicit content into your boy's Mindbank. We don't need another Dissident." He laughed. "I only care about the education being given these days to our children. So tell me, what am I missing?"

I stared at our shadows on the floor, then found myself telling a story:

"EIGHTY-NINE MOONS AGO, I GAVE BIRTH FOR THE FIRST TIME. As a baby, Ren was perfect. I often had to restrain myself not to squeeze his adorable cheeks; his skin was the finest shade of pink. Not long afterwards, my husband came to my bed and suggested that we try for a daughter as well. 'A boy and a girl for balance,' he said.

"I was still recovering in the hospital; when he said this, I seriously considered slapping his face. However, I soon acknowledged that his callousness was not completely his fault. After all, how could I expect a man, having never experienced childbirth, to fully appreciate my suffering? In fact, my husband had not even been present in the operating room, after a doctor had recommended a tasty hotpot restaurant across the street where he could pass the time during my procedure.

"To my surprise, my husband immediately agreed to my proposal—that he relive my experience of giving birth to Ren, as long as I reconsidered my aversion to another pregnancy. He was adamant that I transfer a copy of my memory to him right then, so I humored him as any good Qin wife would. Establishing a connection between our Mindbanks, within seconds I sent him the record of my final hour of labor.

"To my horror, my husband screamed upon opening my download. It did not matter that we were physically in the hospital, that the entire wing could probably hear us. Shamelessly, he cried out vile things, then swore that the memory must have been corrupted. He had the audacity to accuse me of editing the memory to elevate my pain, to cause him harm. As if I were a criminal and not his wife of many moons! Before the doctors removed our son from my womb, my husband had already exited the memory. Then he stormed out, leaving me alone in the hospital room to wonder if I had committed my life to the wrong man . . ."

"NONE OF THIS MAY MAKE MUCH SENSE," I SAID, SUDDENLY LONG-ing for the warm tea that the Elder had offered. "I was never brave enough to ask what he was thinking that day. But after that experience, I realized that I was the one in our marriage who'd have to make the hard decisions."

I did not tell the Elder that as I recounted the story, my Mindbank flashed with images of the first time Ren vomited blood on my robes, the first time that yellow flowers sprouted on his innocent face . . . I did not tell the Elder that because of my boy's mutation—and the genetic records revealing that one of my female ancestors had been a survivor of an early Chrysanthemum Virus outbreak—the Party had asked me to undergo a sterility procedure to ensure I would never infect the gene pool again.

Ren was not only my first child; he would be my only child. It mattered little to me if he grew up ignorant, whether of Party history or social norms. It did not even matter if he were to grow up selfish like his father. The mutation had come from my lineage. It was my fault.

All I wanted was for my boy to be able to grow up. All I wanted was the privilege so many mothers take for granted—that of watching their son become a man.

Why had I chosen to tell that story to this stranger? I had never shared it with anyone before. My head spun as I considered how I might take advantage of my intimate disclosure—but when my mouth opened, I found myself at a loss for words.

Thankfully, the Elder was happy to draw his own meaning from my tale.

"Yes, one's reflections on a memory can easily be as important as the original." The Elder admitted that perhaps my childbirth challenge to my husband was the rare occasion when one could ethically delete a memory, as a preventative measure against future reflections that might lead to violence, or worse, divorce. I did not clarify that my husband had spent most of his moons since Ren's birth traveling for business; the two of us had been separated for a while now, married only on paper to preserve our reputations and the fairy tale of marital stability for our extended families.

"Our Party leaders have even suggested on occasion that I revise *my* Memory Epics!" the Elder announced, as if this were a great affront. "For historians, it's always been a delicate balance—navigating the truth of the past and what is necessary to preserve order in the present . . . Of course, the past cannot be changed, so why take all of it so seriously?"

He chuckled halfheartedly, as if reminded of some criticism he had tried to forget.

Sensing an opening, I confessed that I had once experienced some Memory Content produced by the Elder during his first career as an artisan. Before his Memory Epic about the Incineration of Ri-Ben, I'd heard patriotic stories of our Qin military's might, but to witness the full extent of damage that our Party had inflicted upon a nameless island during the War—it had left me awestruck.

"Is that right?" He did not look pleased, explaining that he was descended from a long line of memory artisans. *The Islander* had been produced by one of his ancestors, and the original had been far more dramatic. Back then, it had been declared a masterpiece, even won an important prize, so the Censors had specially chosen him, out of respect for his family, to revise it into something less visceral. That must have been the version I experienced.

I shuddered to imagine the bloodiness and destruction of the original.

"In their wisdom, our leaders deemed it wiser to phase out the violent aftermath of the War, rather than delete the entire history," the Elder said. "It's the same reason why we are allowed to maintain a semblance of privacy in our Mindbanks, to store memories that we do not wish to upload. The Party is clever in understanding that acceptance is an incremental process, that some freedoms must be preserved even as others are taken away."

Suddenly, the Elder rose gingerly from the table. He raised his hand to prevent me from helping him. "Look there." Our eyes met briefly before he pointed at the crane in the painting. "If I did not draw your attention to it again, I worry that some kindhearted patriot might report it to the Party." The next statement came out as a whisper. "I have a permit for the art, I promise."

Promise? I nearly laughed aloud. Why offer promises when he could have let me review his Mindbank for fidelity? It was the only way to be certain, even if nobody with his rank was required to grant me such access. I stared at the painting again, then thanked him for clearing up the potential misunderstanding.

Slowly I came to accept that I might leave the apartment without figuring out what the man knew, what secrets he might use to threaten my family in the future.

"Such a majestic creature," I noted. "The immortal crane, right?"

A look of surprise came over him. It was the first time I had seen that expression on him, a loss of control.

"You really do possess a stellar education, Ms. Wu."

I blushed, murmuring that the crane had been extinct for only a few hundred moons.

"Still. It does not take long for people to forget."

I gazed at the painting more deeply. How many other details had I missed during our conversation? Beneath the crane's white wings, I noticed a series of long, pale silhouettes. A tiny figure dressed in gray robes, not dissimilar to the Elder's, sat on the crest of the crane's back, likely an Immortal from the Heavenly Palace. I felt an urge to reveal that it was from the old man's Memory Epic that I had discovered the Ri-Ben tradition of folding a thousand paper cranes in exchange for a wish. But then I would need to explain my reasons for folding, so I pushed my desires away. Just as I had pushed away those images of yellow buds sprouting on my boy's face. And the disappointment in his father's eyes when he learned that I had given birth to such imperfection.

If the Elder knew about Ren's illness, and the deal I struck with the Party in exchange for my son's life, he would also know that leaking that information in the Tower would be dangerous for my family, leading to potential retaliation from one of our neighbors.

Before my fears could overtake me, the old man unexpectedly launched into a confession. Long ago, there had been a woman in his life, the Elder said. She had been brilliant, the sister of a colleague who had worked on the Ri-Ben content. They had admired each other greatly; yet he had been unable to promise her a family, given the demands of his profession.

"Her face resembles yours actually," the Elder said, a sad smile flitting across his face. "She was a kind soul. I heard she passed away a few moons ago. I sometimes wonder whether she forgave me in the end."

It was then that I realized I was sitting while the Elder was not.

"Will you come with Ren next time?" he asked. Standing with his arms spread as if to balance his fragile body, the old man trembled in the emptiness between me and the door.

Did he already know our secrets? Panicked, I felt a sudden urge to leave. It was too much . . . No, the Elder did not want to sleep with me; he was not such a simple man . . . So what did he want from us? To feel the semblance of a family? Even if it were the mere shadow of one? As atonement for his failures, perhaps with that deceased lover?

It was impossible to tell. The last pretense of politeness gone, I edged past the Elder and out the door, wondering all the while whether he deserved my cruel suspicions:

I'm sorry, but I cannot help you.

I cannot afford to trust, not when the only thing of value I can offer the Party is the misplaced faith of our neighbors. If any of them learnt of Ren's illness and suspected our betrayal of that good man, then we would no longer be safe in the Tower.

No, I can never bring him again. I must remember my duty. For my son awaits at home, and he is the only innocent here.

LATER, WHEN REN ASKED, "MOMMY, WHY ARE YOU SAD?" I EXplained that all the birds I had described from the historian's painting were dead, no longer flying in the heavenly skies.

My son asked me many other questions too—about the winter migratory patterns of birds before the War, the mass extinctions catalyzed by Western climate change—but I soon realized that it was not safe to discuss the cranes anymore, not when the artist was likely of Ri-Ben descent, and not when the Elder may have lied about owning a permit.

I had been a fool not to check his memories.

Instead, I whispered in my son's ear how grateful I was that the two of us were lying in bed together, safe. And when the boy tilted his head in confusion, I stared into his brown eyes, relieved that the skin on his face was as clear as milk, devoid of any yellow flowers or poisons that had long ago infected his mother's weak, weak heart.

+86 SHANGHAI

Jiahong

"Chinaman, money? Got any green on you?"

Jiahong shifted his gaze to the red Coca-Cola billboards and narrow windows overhead, everywhere save for the unfamiliar Black man standing by the payphone. It had only been five months since he boarded the plane for America, and he was still new to the customs of these people living in the city oddly known as the Big Apple. He adjusted his glasses and wiped the sweat off his nose. Just as his dishwasher friend had taught him, Jiahong avoided eye contact with everyone he crossed in Manhattan.

"You here to make a call?" the man said, his T-shirt soaked by the summer heat as he smoked beside the empty phone booth. Dropping his cigarette butt, the man crushed it against the pavement with his heel. "China, right? Don't stress, you're in the right place."

Jiahong took a deep breath. After getting lost in a maze of alleys for the last half hour, he was relieved to have found one of the small-time criminals he had only heard stories about—men who leaned against payphones and made international calls for immigrants at a steep discount using stolen phone cards.

Steadying his hands, Jiahong passed over ten one-dollar bills fastened by a pink rubber band. He pointed at the top bill, where he had scrawled his wife's number in blue ink.

The stranger began to dial.

ON THE FIRST SNOWFALL LAST YEAR, JIAHONG LEFT HIS WIFE
Little Jade and their young son in Shanghai to make his fortune
in one of America's famous Chinatowns, having finally borrowed
enough money from his friends and relatives to afford the flight and
visa fees.

In New York, he wrote faithfully to his wife every week. Rain
or shine, he spent his days pedaling on a borrowed bicycle to deliver
General Tso's Chicken to affluent families on the Upper East Side.
He tried not to lie too often in his letters; he preferred to focus on
the positives of American life—like how there was a magical subway connecting the city, or how the tap water did not need to be
boiled here, although he used his kettle anyway. Still, he could tell
from his wife's letters that she was struggling without him, even if
she would never admit her loneliness.

*Will you write your mother and ask her to stop visiting? It is
difficult enough to raise your son alone, without having to nod
along to her criticisms.*

In the small phone booth, Jiahong tightened his fists. He longed
to hear his family's voices in Shanghainese, so much warmer than
the cacophony of dialects spoken by his compatriots who worked
at First Wok. Worse, the English he heard here sounded nothing
like the pronunciations he had carefully memorized from text-
books. Until he arrived, he had assumed that most New Yorkers
were white, differing only in the paleness of their skin tones; now
on his deliveries, he would notice himself being overwhelmed by the
multitude of ethnicities on the streets.

As he waited for the stranger to finish dialing, he began to worry
that his wife might be angry. This would be his first time calling,
and he had forgotten to remind her of the time difference. When he
realized his mistake, it was already too late to send another letter.

What if she had spent all night waiting by her mother's phone?

"Five thousand yuan a month to ride your bicycle across the
city—why not remind her, if she starts yelling?" the dishwasher at

First Wok advised. "Think of how many red-bean cakes that would buy your son!"

Jiahong frequently parroted the dishwasher's truisms in his letters to Little Jade. But sometimes he would write a second letter that recounted the truth—that he was far from thriving in this foreign place. On occasion, he felt stabs of resentment, not only toward the wealthy Taiwanese immigrants he heard on the streets but also his Fujianese coworkers who, despite having arrived on boats and lacking education, were often hardier and better suited to the physical labor required in restaurants. Unwilling to throw any of the pages away, he would slide his guilty secrets beneath the mattress he had purchased from the previous tenant, an Indian immigrant with whom he had communicated through gestures. Beside the letters, Jiahong hid his restaurant tips, held together by thin rubber bands.

When he felt lonely, he would press his face against the mattress and voice his fears to his small stash of savings. Then he would laugh bitterly, as if to ridicule himself and the notion that those green bills might be able to listen, and perhaps even empathize.

AS SOON AS THE BLACK MAN STOPPED DIALING HIS WIFE'S NUMber, Jiahong reached for the receiver. He gripped the cold metal with his fists. "Little Jade? Are you living well?"

"Ma told me to talk about monkeys. Their red bums."

"Bird! Good heavens—" Hearing his son's voice made tears swell in Jiahong's eyes. He quickly wiped them, so the stranger leaning now against the brick wall wouldn't notice and take advantage by charging him more for the call.

"Did Ma take you to the zoo? Did you see the lions and tigers?"

Silence. He imagined his son hiding behind Little Jade's slim frame, as if he were some unfamiliar uncle from the countryside. "Bird? It's your father. Remember me?"

He heard fumbling as his wife came on the line.

"Did he mention the baboons yet?" Her voice was hoarse, making him wonder if she had just gotten out of bed. "He was chasing them yesterday as if he was part of the troop."

Was she sick? But if he asked and Little Jade admitted it, what comfort could he offer? "The New York dogs live in luxury!" Jiahong blurted instead, sticking to his library of rehearsed tales. "They sleep in their own rooms, bigger than mine!"

As he waited for her answer, he imagined Little Jade's gentle laughter, the beauty spot trembling on her left cheek.

"Is this call expensive?" she asked. "How many minutes can we talk?"

"Oh, there is a deal." Through the plastic pane of the phone booth, Jiahong stared at the stranger. "You won't believe who dialed your number, Little Jade."

Had she even seen a photograph of a Black man before? He watched the flame glow at the end of the man's cigarette, illuminating the long ropes of hair around his unshaven features. As the cigarette flickered once more, Jiahong felt a hint of envy as he stared at the stranger's broad shoulders, relaxed above his sweat-ridden T-shirt.

"We cannot afford such calls, Jiahong. Better to save money until you can pay off the debt we owe to your family."

A lump formed in his throat. "Is this the most important thing to discuss? It's the first time we've talked in months."

"I have responded to every letter. Is that not enough?" Her voice cracked on the line; he wondered whether it was simply a phone issue or whether she was irritated with him. "You wrote that this is an important time for you, when you need to be focused on earning money."

"It is." Jiahong tried to slow his breathing. "That is not a lie."

"Do you want me to reassure you? To tell you that I know it is not easy over there? I can do that. If that is what you need."

He wanted to slam the receiver against the hook, holding back only because he did not want to waste the green bills he had already paid the stranger. Instead, he took a deep breath and swallowed the wave of criticisms rising from his throat.

"I am disappointed that you did not ask if I was living well, wife," he said softly. "It is lonely here. Maybe I cannot survive any longer in this city without hearing your voice."

As he waited for his confession to sink in, Jiahong felt their precious time slipping away, each minute another invisible coin disappearing down the mouth of a storm gutter.

AFTER THE FIRST CALL, JIAHONG RETURNED TO THE SAME PHONE booth every month.

"Did you know that your mother has been spying on me?" Little Jade asked three months later, as soon as she answered. Jiahong winced. He had hoped to discuss something pleasant—how he had recently made a new friend, a chef who had stowed away on a boat from Southeast Asia and was cooking Chinese food for the first time. He hated when their precious conversations began with complaints, especially when her issues were valid, and he could not simply dismiss them.

"Last week, your mother asked why I brought your son to the Peace Hotel!"

Jiahong heard Bird stomping in the background, mimicking the cries of martial artists in a duel. He imagined the boy's arms waving wildly, brandishing an invisible sword.

"I met with your university classmate to hand him mooncakes to bring to America. Did you receive them yet? His flight must have arrived over the weekend. Never mind," Little Jade said. "Your mother interrogated Bird! She accused me of having an affair!"

Jiahong lowered the receiver and rubbed the knots along his back. Three weeks ago, he had fallen off his bicycle during a thunderstorm. Some of the Styrofoam boxes had tumbled onto the street and the family who had ordered them were unmoved by his pleas in broken English to pay for the food.

"Did I marry a mute? Are you listening, Jiahong?"

"Bad connection. Sorry."

"Don't you care, Jiahong? Are you ever going to bring us over?" Her voice grew louder when she became angry. "Or do you have a new family over there?"

"Don't be foolish." He did not want to encourage her paranoia. Wrapping his fingers around the metal cord, he squeezed in frustration. "I'll write to my mother. Promise."

"Promise? What is your promise worth? Can you promise me this? If I were no longer alive, would you bring Bird to America?"

Did she really believe that he would send for them if she threatened to harm herself? He pushed down his anger, not wanting to prolong their argument.

"The Black man is coming," Jiahong lied.

"Have you no heart? You wouldn't entrust Bird to your mother, would you?"

"I am out of time, wife. He is coming to charge more money." Without another warning, Jiahong returned the cold receiver to its latch. Directing his anger toward the one person nearby, he glared at the Black man smoking against the brick wall.

To Jiahong's surprise, the man waved at him and smiled. Almost as if they were friends.

"LET'S SEPARATE," HE SAID.

A sentence Jiahong had never uttered during their year apart.

"Yes, the marriage is too difficult," she answered.

But this conversation only played out in his mind, and in the letters he wrote but never sent. On his long subway rides back to Queens each night, Jiahong wrote pages upon pages, enough to assemble a novel.

"I sacrificed everything for you and Bird," he wrote. "How can you not recognize that? Why is it so impossible for you to understand my struggles?"

On occasion, Jiahong wondered about the stories of his countrymen slumped against the nearby seats. Surely there were some who had tasted even more bitterness than he; perhaps they owed debts to snakeheads who had smuggled them across the ocean. How many had also left their families behind? Yet, Jiahong knew that they all looked the same to the pale rulers of this country, those men and women incapable of distinguishing his tan from the jaundice that now suffused his tired face.

"BIRD IS FEELING BETTER," LITTLE JADE SAID. "THE WORST OF HIS illness has passed."

"Good." More than a year had elapsed since their first call. They had settled into a routine of talking only about what happened that month, rather than revisiting old arguments. To his relief, after he began sending more money home, his wife sounded less anxious now about the cost of every passing minute they spent on the phone.

"My friends, the couple in Queens, offered us their yellow table," Jiahong said, "For when you and Bird come." He failed to mention that the wooden table was chipped, or that he had helped the husband carry it from a refuse pile. In bed at night, he still occasionally cursed the Indian for selling him a mattress that he could have gotten for free on garbage day.

"Your son has missed a lot of school—I had to piggyback him across the bridge to Renmin Hospital last weekend. He insisted that we bring his school blanket to the hospital. He asked for a duckling patch, so I sewed it onto the blanket while he was asleep, to remind him how special he is."

Hearing a tap, Jiahong turned to see the Black man slapping the phone booth with his palm, waving a green bill in the air. Jiahong shook his head. He had paid for thirty minutes; surely no more than twenty had passed. Only upon checking his watch did Jiahong realize that his conversation had gone over. He lowered his head apologetically. As he received a grin through the pane, Jiahong wondered why neither of them had bothered to ask for the other's name.

"Are you listening?" Little Jade said, "Your son keeps getting ill!"

"Didn't you say he was better?—"

"Six thousand yuan a month? What is the point of money if you cannot take care of your son?"

Jiahong lowered the receiver for a moment of respite before deciding how to respond.

"I will bring you over soon." Clearing his throat, he repeated the words more confidently, not wanting to reveal any hint of his fear that the new owners at First Wok might soon replace him and his colleagues with an outsourced delivery service. "I will bring you both over. I am telling the truth."

Little Jade exhaled deeply on the other end.

Did his wife believe him? Before he could ruin the moment, Jiahong heard a dramatic sigh on the line, too exaggerated to have come from his wife.

"Stop it," Little Jade reprimanded. "I'm talking to your father"; only then did Jiahong realize that it had been Bird mimicking his mother. Suddenly, his wife began to giggle, reminding Jiahong of the carefree young woman he had fallen in love with years ago. Then all three of them broke out in laughter, one family separated by seven thousand miles.

Little Jade

At the market near City God Temple, where she haggled each week for vegetables and fruits, Little Jade walked among the stalls, inspecting the freshness of each bundle of greens. Between pondering what dishes she could make for her parents and son that evening, she let her thoughts drift toward what she should discuss with her husband on their next call.

"Should we bring your mother and father a larger gift for Mid-Autumn Festival this year?" Little Jade considered asking. "Can you send a bit more money this month?"

She shook her head, discomfited by the idea of demanding more from Jiahong, whom she knew was already working seventy hours a week at the restaurant to support them. But no matter how much she tried to explain Jiahong's situation to his parents, she knew they had built up unrealistic expectations of their son's wealth and success in America. She also accepted that her husband was too proud to ever tell them the truth of his hardships.

In front of her, Bird was weaving through the market stalls before stopping at the butcher's stand. Although the chunks of fatty pork made her mouth water, she grabbed her son's hand to lead him away.

"Mama, can we buy some milk candy today?"

Little Jade laughed, then nodded as her son exclaimed in delight. Releasing his hand, she let him run ahead to their favorite sweets stall, where the auntie would be more than happy to look after him.

"Will our son resent us one day? For taking him away from Shanghai?" As Little Jade watched her son skip across the market, she could not help but revisit the secret conversation she often conducted in her head. She knew how her husband would respond.

"What? For bringing him to America? Where the sky is blue and the air is clean? Where he will not need to study sixteen hours every day to prepare for the college exam?" Jiahong would shake his head, she was sure of it. "Never, foolish wife."

"We will separate him. From his friends. From my parents, who treat him like a treasure. You know that my parents are not as young as yours."

"Will he complain when he earns ten times the salary? Did you not complain that he has been throwing the cushions like a wild animal? He is a boy. He knows nothing."

She knew he would ignore her worries about her parents. At that moment, she reminded herself that she needed to bring her stubborn father to the dentist soon; if his toothache did not get better, she would have to cook their family only stews for the next month, no matter how much Bird enjoyed her sweet-and-sour pork ribs.

In her imagination, Little Jade heard sirens screaming in the distance from Jiahong's end of the line. It did not help that he often mentioned the Black man who dialed their calls. His name was Wilson, as if those foreign syllables were supposed to make Little Jade feel safer. Apparently, there were so many broken windows in New York that the police had created a new policy to arrest anyone who didn't repair their homes quickly enough.

"Shanghai is changing," she could say. "We built our first subway line. The French supermarket also opened last week. Three thousand people waited to ride the escalators."

She did not mention how proud she was of having raised Bird in her husband's absence. Recently, his kindergarten teacher had praised her for nurturing their son's enthusiasm in math, after she began to tutor Bird at night. How could she teach her son right from wrong in America, where she would be unable to communicate with the teachers if he misbehaved?

Yet she expected her husband to have the last word. "Don't you want to reunite our family? Cure our boy's asthma? Aren't you the one always asking when I can bring our son over?"

Fair enough. And so she never raised the question, unable to bear the resentment in his voice or forgive his inability to hear the anxiety beneath her words.

Slapping the overripe belly of a watermelon, Little Jade reached for some peaches at the back of the stall. She smiled at the sunburnt fruit seller behind the counter, whom she had trained through their negotiations to offer her his best price from the beginning.

Would Bird miss these sweet peaches too? Would he resent her if the shops there did not sell the milk candies that he adored?

No, Little Jade admitted. It was she who would struggle to leave, to abandon all that was familiar to join her husband in his new home.

Bird

Many years passed.

Long after the boy had given up his Chinese passport, Bird sat alone in his dorm room following the end of his third semester at Dartmouth. His roommate had already moved out, and he was dreading the prospect of fitting everything he owned into two suitcases and relocating to a temporary apartment for the summer. Lying on his twin mattress, he tried to avoid staring at the stripped bed and plaster walls on the other side of the room, as if ignorance would protect him from the loneliness.

His cellphone buzzed. Sitting up, Bird flipped it open.

"Son, you make us proud!" his father shouted in his accented English. The boy winced and moved the phone farther from his ear. He knew that his father was calling from a banquet hall, likely with a tomato-red face from drinking too much baijiu. "170 on LSAT! So what if there is no guarantee for law school? Think positive and write good essay."

Bird sighed. Although it was the weekend of his father's twenty-fifth college reunion, his parents had been calling him nonstop from Shanghai, excited to find out his score on the law school admissions exam he had taken last month. More than anything, Bird saw his score as a relief, even if he had secretly hoped to do better.

"Thanks, Dad. Enjoy your reunion. Just don't embarrass me by telling everyone."

His father chuckled. "I did not own one suit when I go to America! Now my son will make big money as lawyer. What joy!"

Bird heard his mother fumbling for the phone. "Your father drink too much at reception," she said. "Too little food. Too much talk."

"I know every word I say! I congratulate my son!" His father had recovered the phone. "How far we come! It was so difficult. Your mother worried I leave you both in China. When I take subway to Manhattan to meet Wilson at payphone, every call—she so unhappy!"

His voice was deafening. Bird groaned at the mention of his father's one Black friend after fifteen years of living in America, a recurring character in their family's immigrant stories. He vaguely recalled his father mentioning that they had lost touch, after Wilson rediscovered God and became consumed by his church duties.

He heard his mother wrestling for the phone again.

"Do not listen to Father. All you need remember is talk about family in essay. Many hard years in New York. We fight together!" she said. "I repeat, do not write like last essay. So shy."

Bird took a deep breath. His parents believed that he should have written his undergraduate college admission essays about their family's journey to America rather than his penultimate season on the high school basketball team. While his essays mentioned that Bird had been the only Asian player on the court, they had centered on a locker-room conflict that he'd resolved as the team captain, rather than anything about being a first-generation immigrant.

If you write better story, maybe you go to Harvard!

Months after his acceptances to lesser schools, his parents still regularly brought up the missed opportunity, until he began to wonder if they were disappointed by their absence in his essays. Perhaps they thought that Bird wasn't proud enough of their sacrifices. It wasn't until he was admitted off Dartmouth's waitlist, and they took a family picture all wearing Big Green sweatshirts, that his parents' comments subsided. Later that autumn, they called to explain that they were returning to Shanghai to be closer to his mother's parents, their tone strongly implying that they were setting an example so that Bird too might prioritize his filial duties one day. He wasn't particularly excited by the prospect of visiting Shanghai, no matter how many times his father repeated that his birthplace was the city of the future. Despite his father's pride, the truth was that their ancestors weren't even from Shanghai: his paternal line was descended from a village near Wuhan more famous for an armless swimmer than anything else.

It had been a long time since Bird had been back to China. When his parents recently showed him photographs of the new Shanghai skyline from the Bund, he scarcely recognized the city where he had grown up.

"I'll do my best on the essay," Bird grumbled. "Now, let Dad enjoy himself and give me time to pack." He scoffed, not wanting to believe that either Harvard or Yale wanted to read yet another essay perpetuating the myth of the model minority. Then again, he could not deny that his parents had several friends whose children had unabashedly highlighted their challenges with race in essays, while removing stereotypically Asian activities such as chess from their resumes. Many of them had indeed been accepted into better schools than Dartmouth.

All his parents were asking was for him to pen a few words of hyperbole. Was that too much to ask? He could have easily written about the summer they had been evicted from their apartment on Elmhurst, his fear and confusion when his parents hurriedly packed up his toys without explanation. For the next month, the three of them had slept shoulder to shoulder in a family friend's living room. What about the time his mother nearly died from her burst appendix? When Bird closed his eyes and concentrated, he could still hear her screams that night from the expensive taxi she took to the public hospital.

Or were his parents referring to the stories they had told him of their struggles before Bird arrived in America? Stories that were largely true, as he discovered the Christmas before they left for China, when he returned home to help them pack and found a box of dusty letters beneath their bed. It took him a long time to translate everything, and even longer to figure out why many of them featured the same dates. Nevertheless, the smudged pages had illuminated many mysteries—from the resentment he witnessed in his mother's eyes whenever his father boasted about his early immigrant days to the way she pulled away whenever his father's hands came too close. Had it not been for Bird and the Chinese stigma against divorce, he felt that his mother and father might have long separated.

"Son, where you go? We cannot hear."

Bird's throat tightened upon recalling the letters, as if the phone in his hand had transformed into a dark cord, twisting taut around his neck.

"Outside, we go outside, then call!"

His mother hung up. As Bird listened to the shriek of the broken dial tone, he stared across his empty room. When did he last believe his parents when they said they were proud of him? No matter what words they used now, he struggled to imagine ever justifying what they had given up for his future.

He waited for her to call. When she did, he knew that he would protest and pretend to ignore their advice. Then he would quietly bury his pride—just as his father had with those unsent letters years ago—and write the essay that everyone seemed to want.

As his phone began to buzz, Bird imagined his father standing before some nondescript payphone and calling them during that first summer abroad, his T-shirt soaked with sweat from biking around Manhattan and infused with the stench of recycled sesame oil from First Wok.

If they could go back in time, would they still choose to immigrate, knowing everything they did now? The boy shook his head. To succeed in this promised land that his parents had worked so hard to reach, he would agree to whatever it asked of him—and everyone would be happier for it.

Wasn't that what mattered in the end?

THIRD MESSAGE

 at ▮▮ : ▮▮▮▮

Lately, I have been fantasizing about fatherhood.

If I had the chance at a second life, even if it were in a carbon-composite body with the same memories, I would want to raise a family. A boy, maybe. Every night, I would tell him a new bedtime story, different from the ones my mother told. Maybe I could learn to sew too, so that I could stitch the outlines of his favorite animals onto his robes—saber-tooth tigers, a red-crowned crane—whatever he wanted, so long as he asked politely.

In my imagination, he is never old enough to take the Gaokao, never too embarrassed to embrace his father. I recognize that this is nothing more than self-indulgence; nevertheless, I promise that I would never be like those traitors from before the War, who left their families behind in Qin to pursue better prospects abroad. I'd treat fatherhood as a privilege. I am sure of it; even if it no longer makes sense, given my present situation, to connect my Mindbank to any online marriage market in search of a life partner. Still, even as I wait for the Red Guards to appear at my door, there remains a small glimmer of hope that when it's all said and done, the Party might one day release me. Then there would be no reason why I couldn't become a father, grateful to live with more intention than when I believed I had all the time in the world.

Hope.

Since receiving these memories, that has been the hardest thing to handle. The fantasy of freedom, even when deep down I know that there is no universe in which the Party would let me go. Yet every time I reexperience my inheritance, I invent more excuses for why the Epics are not subversive. For instance, despite its references to the Incineration of Ri-Ben, hadn't *The Islander* won a prize in its time? Or the mother in *Innocents*—she demonstrated steadfast loyalty to the Party by reporting the Dissident in her Tower! Even *After the Bloom*—was it so bad for modern Qin citizens to learn that the Party once sacrificed a few towns to prevent the spread of the Chrysanthemum Virus? The decision likely saved millions, as acknowledged by the narrator of the Epic.

Certain memories in the inheritance, such as the tale of the armless swimmer, were not even banned until recent moons, when the Censors became more sensitive about any mention of disabilities within Qin's perfect population. Of course, it has always been the Party's prerogative to periodically redefine the borders of what is acceptable in our Mindbanks.

I'm going mad. I guess that's what a secret hope can do.

Allow me to make a confession then—that hope is also why I have been holding out, too afraid to share the most subversive of my mother's memories with you.

Recently, my desperation brought me back to the storms from my childhood. I suffered from nightmares of my small body suspended midair in the rain and lightning, buffeted by relentless wind while my arms flailed helplessly. I was surprised to discover that even in my dreams, my nature was to keep fighting, to stay alive against all odds.

Only, survival is impossible for me now. Had there been merely one or two problematic memories in my inheritance, perhaps I could have pled guilty and sworn my fealty to the Party to receive a lighter sentence, but to be found in possession of such a large collection— the courts would judge it an unforgivable offense, no matter how I spun my excuses.

I cannot sleep anymore. I live only to await the Red Guards. It is inevitable. For as soon as the Censors review my inheritance, they will come. And as my mind becomes consumed by the infinite unknowns—

of my impending sentence, of the exact day of reckoning—I realize that I cannot endure another moon in such anxiety. It is too late. Because Mindbanks are designed to withstand almost any damage, even if I leapt tonight from the roof of my Tower, the scientists could still Reincarnate me via my device. A suicide attempt would only shine a spotlight on my guilt, before they made me serve out my punishment from the Qin courts.

So I wish to face the consequences now.

Yes. Rather than living in fear, clinging onto my last moments of freedom, allow me to transfer these final memories from my mother, including the ones most damning of our leaders in power. So that the true histories of Qin may be preserved.

Even if I never dreamed of revolution in my lifetime.

PROMISED LAND

I t is strange, the way you came to me in a dream.

The Desert. I was dragging myself across a dune when you appeared, more vivid than the organs I pictured melting inside of me. For the first time in our friendship, I imagined outscoring you on an exam and earning a nod of approval from my father.

Where was Ba now? It didn't matter. All I needed was to keep moving forward. Onward and upward; there was no point in looking back.

With every step in the sand, my mind sank deeper into the haze.

DO YOU REMEMBER OUR SUNDAYS?

How we used to set the day aside for church and watch the Reverend stumble onto the stage, whispering bets in each other's ear about whether he'd be able to stay standing for the entire sermon? One week, he forgot what he planned to preach and repeated the same Bible verses about surrender and faith from two sermons earlier. Everyone clapped politely; only you and I were mean enough to snicker.

That was a typical weekend before the War. When the two of us were growing up, before they came up with another name for our neighborhood.

Pinch me. Just like you used to do on Sundays so that Ba wouldn't catch me sleeping. Pinch me, go on. So when I open my eyes, I might see you sitting next to me in the pew struggling not to laugh at another of the Reverend's metaphors—like when he compared God's all-seeing eye to Big Brother from *1984*. Or to the 500 million cameras installed in Qin to spy on its own citizens. Oh, if all we had to worry about were cameras.

Nobody seemed to care that the Reverend's sermons were offensive. Maybe it was his droning voice. Maybe it was the snail's pace of his lectures, although that may have helped Ba follow the English. Otherwise, he may never have understood enough to accept Jesus as his Savior. Not that the Ten Commandments, nor any other passage from the Bible, ever saved me from the flat of my father's palm when he heard my breath growing shallow on Sundays.

"Boys with yellow skin cannot get benefit from affirmative action," Ba liked to remind me. He tried to motivate me to study harder by saying that you'd be the one getting into an Ivy League, as if that would've been a tragedy rather than something worth celebrating.

If you were here, you'd remind me that you were only Black by virtue of the one-drop rule; I still remember your father's pale face in that Polaroid tucked in your wallet, the snapshot of the man who abandoned you. But none of that matters. Because to anybody who doesn't think of you like a brother, you're just another Black kid from Queens.

My father liked you. Did you know that? It may not have been obvious when Ba drove you to our place after church to study. But as soon as you walked out the door, he'd go on and on about your work ethic, how you kept your grades high despite the leg up he was certain you'd get from colleges. And of course there was the fact that you never missed a Sunday service, rarely a wrinkle on that white dress shirt you wore to sermons every week.

When my parents got married in Qin, my father was still working as a mechanical engineer for the Party. Until then, he had done everything right: scored high enough on the Gaokao to enroll in a top university; got a job in the same government building as my mother. So when he decided that he wanted to take my mother and me out of the country—to America, no less!—she and her family were stunned. They had all heard the rumors that leaving Qin might become a crime in the future, a betrayal of the homeland. My mother asked for time to consider the move, but as months passed, she only came up with more reasons to delay. Deep down, I think Ba always knew that my mother wasn't someone who could just up and leave everything she'd ever known. Perhaps that's why he told me not to blame her, as if I could just be like him and squeeze the emotions out of myself with an iron fist.

Your work ethic probably reminded him of himself.

"When I am your age, I study sixteen hours every day for three years before my Gaokao," Ba said. "My wrist get bruise from writing against desk!"

I remember when my father first explained the Gaokao to you. Ten million students taking a single exam to determine their fates, neither school grades nor personal statements considered. I worried that you wouldn't understand. I worried that you would stare at me like you used to do whenever the Reverend launched into another tirade about our Christian duty to raise legions of God-fearing children, or the life lessons he'd gleaned from selling phone cards on the streets before reclaiming his relationship with the Lord.

Because how could you begin to grasp the importance of that test, so revered by every Qin citizen? Could you believe that every year before the two-day exam, the world's largest nation would halt all construction and station policemen by every school to direct traffic and minimize noise? What about the parents who hired full-time nannies with college degrees to ensure their teenagers were studying every waking hour? Or the armies of Party drones circling overhead on those two critical days, electronically monitoring for cheaters. Why the national divorce rate skyrockets every year after the test—the result of thousands of parents who gritted their teeth to stay together, so as not to risk distracting their child before that all-important exam.

But I was wrong. Because you did understand. Because you had long understood the odds of succeeding in the so-called meritocracy of America, and you knew you needed to be twice as good to get half the credit.

My best friend. How could I have gotten everything so wrong about you?

IN OUR OLD NEIGHBORHOOD, THE YMCA WAS REPURPOSED INTO a Great Hall of Examinations. Thankfully, it's not far from the Fourth World orphanage where the Party keeps us kids without families after the War, so I was allowed to simply walk over for my exam.

It was my first attempt at the Gaokao, not that I'd be allowed a retake. Then again, it's the first year that the Party has extended the exam to Qin-Americans, so maybe that's too early to say. You were gone by the time the YMCA shut down, right? When the Qin military came to inspect our neighborhood, the building had been sitting empty for so long that being repurposed for the Gaokao wasn't such a shabby fate.

By the time I arrived at the soccer field outside the exam center, there was a crowd clamoring outside the doors. Most of them looked my age, no older than twenty. While some were scheduled to take the exam that day, I knew that others were only there to gather intel. Unlike previous iterations, the Gaokao no longer involved memorization, so it did not need to be conducted synchronously as had been done in the past. Although I knew that some boys at the orphanage had already taken the exam, I didn't feel close enough to any of them to ask about their experience.

Every ten minutes, one of the Qin techs would open the center doors and call out a string of names. As I waited in the soccer field, filled with weeds and dirt after all the grass died from neglect, I examined the new hall. Besides the generator humming outside the entrance, I didn't notice many differences from the old YMCA. Of course, it didn't make sense for Qin to invest heavily in these test centers, not when they needed to retrofit thousands of buildings across their colonies for the Gaokao. At least the Qin military regularly cleared the garbage around the center. There were rumors that most of the affluent neighborhoods in Washington, DC, had become dilapidated, home to mountains of litter that grew taller every day, and shards of broken glass on the sidewalks from the damaged buildings. Thankfully, the Qin military had not bothered to vandalize the poorer suburbs when they assumed control of our city.

Eventually, one of the techs called my name and ushered a group of us inside the center. We were asked to move quickly, passing rusty water fountains and dust-framed squares on the floor where I recalled vending machines once stood. After walking through a pair of swinging doors, we soon found ourselves inside an immense rectangular room under a glass ceiling.

Sunlight poured in from above. The space was filled with giant stacks of servers wired to helmets worn by dozens of Qin-American teenagers, each reclining in a faux leather chair. The silence unnerved me; I was not used to people being so quiet. A few of them looked calm, as if asleep, but most were gasping, chests heaving up and down, as if bearing witness to atrocities. The whites of their eyes stared blankly at me. I began counting to ten in English and then in Qin to steady my breath. Before long, a tech strapped me into one of the chairs. Placing a red helmet over my head, she began running diagnostics on a monitor. Even with my restricted field of vision, I could see lines of code flashing across the tech's screen.

My eyes flicked along the blue-and-white mosaic tiles along the walls. Something about the room made me think that I had been here before. As the answer eluded me, I tried to distract myself by counting the number of tiles in each row.

"Sorry, this takes a bit of time," the tech said. "I'll get you inside the simulation soon enough." I felt a tinge of relief that Ba had taught me enough of the Qin language to understand her. "Although if you had a Mindbank, it would've been easier to set this up at home."

Who in the Fourth World could afford a Mindbank? I tried to hide my disbelief, knowing that even in Qin, the technology was largely restricted to Party officials and their scions. If not for her job, this tech would never have had access to such a device.

I pursed my lips. Perhaps she assumed that I was better off because of the color of my skin. Certainly I considered myself privileged compared to the white boys who had been dispatched to the reeducation camps. It was harder to judge whether I was luckier than the Black and Brown boys in the room, given my father's abandonment of Qin so long ago.

Staring at the blue-and-white tiles, I suddenly realized that this room was where the swimming pool used to be; they must have filled it in with concrete. The glass ceiling should've been enough to clue me in, but I was never too smart, I guess.

"I'm sure you already know this, but I have to give you the full lecture." The tech's eyes began to glaze over, a side-effect of accessing one's Mindbank. "Upon entering the simulation, you will be assigned an avatar that befits your legal status. You will use that digital avatar to navigate across the Gaokao," she said in a monotone voice. "Note that the terrain will change as you progress. Although you are not expected to finish the race, you will be rewarded for whatever distance you do complete . . . Time will pass differently in the simulation, but do not worry about dinner . . . At the end of the examination season, your Gaokao score will be posted, along with the assignment to your Party office of indefinite employment."

I nodded, even though the tech couldn't see. If I wanted to build myself a better life in this new world, I needed to excel at this exam. An exceptional score might be the only way I'd see my father again: if the Gaokao determined that I had high worth as a worker and held some tangible value to Qin's economic future, surely the Party would consider my request?

The tech's eyes blinked and refocused, signaling the end of the lecture. She turned toward me. "Shall we?" She didn't allow me time to respond. "Let's begin."

The room began to swirl. A moment later, I felt myself stumbling inside my avatar in the simulation. Before I could familiarize myself with the body, I realized that I was sinking into pitch-black sludge. Goose bumps appeared on my new arms.

Accept it. This is your body now.

The sky spun, as I sank deeper into the mud.

The Swamp, I realized. I was starting my exam in the Swamp.

My arms flailed to keep myself above the muck. Upon seeing two hands, I let loose a sigh of relief, even as mud seeped into my mouth. When I tried kicking, however, I realized that something was missing. Impossible. Grabbing onto a floating log, I managed to hold on until I reached solid ground. Once I dragged myself onto some hard dirt, I rolled onto my back. How could I already be exhausted? I tried splaying my legs but when I reached out to feel my left leg, all my fingers grasped was air.

The Party had given me a deficient avatar as punishment for my father's crime.

I would need to run the whole Gaokao on one leg. I marveled at the virtual handicap they had given me. Not that I hadn't expected one, but this was so literal.

I should have known. Long before Qin renamed itself, the best universities in China always reserved fewer places for rural students. Wasn't it finally time for those kids from Qin to get ahead? Even if we in the Fourth World were the ones getting shafted this round.

Flipping onto my stomach, I muttered a prayer. Bracing my arms against the earth, I stared into the horizon. The Swamp seemed endless. I would need to survive a multitude of sinkholes just to advance to the next stage.

Did I stand a chance?

Still, what choice did I have but to keep moving?

I began to crawl.

BY THE TIME YOU AND I BECAME FRIENDS, YOUR MOTHER WAS gone.

We were thirteen and reviewing a chemistry problem set in my bedroom, the only time we truly talked about her. Bored by diagrams of covalent bonds, I tried to catch your attention.

"I'm so bored. Haven't we studied enough?" I asked. "Ms. Ford said that she'd drop our lowest quiz score. Let's text some girls."

You were sitting on my bed, propped against the wall. I waited for your eyes to lift from your purple binder as a savory aroma drifted into the room, likely Ba frying some onions in the kitchen for his salted fish and chicken rice.

"Come on! I don't want to hole up all year studying," I said. My plastic desk chair screeched as I stood abruptly. "Look, man, I don't want to die a virgin."

Your laughter filled the room. "The ladies will come," you promised. As you stretched your thick arms toward the ceiling, I watched your biceps flex, then loosen.

"Patience, man," you said. "Patience."

If only I had those muscles; for a while now, I'd found it maddening that none of the girls I crushed on seemed to mind that you were a nerd. The same girls who ignored my texts would invite you to the mall, mistaking your shyness for a sign of maturity.

"That's easy for you to say. Remember how good your dad looked?" I blurted. "Stick your head in the kitchen and you'll see what my genes have in store for me."

As soon as the words left my mouth, I saw your frozen expression. Reflexively, I reached across my bed to touch your arm in apology.

"Sorry, I didn't mean to be a jerk . . ."

To my surprise, your forearm was clenched, tighter than I could have imagined. I didn't expect such a strong reaction, given how much time had passed since your father disappeared. Slowly, I released my grip when you met my eyes again.

"Did I ever tell you why I started studying so hard?" you asked.

I shook my head. Were your eyes always so brown? What else had I failed to notice about you?

"You know how after Ma died, my aunt took me in. Well, she didn't have the heart to tell a six-year-old that his mom and dad were gone, so she said they'd gone on a trip. Somewhere so far away that our phones couldn't reach them.

"She promised that if I got straight A's for five years, she'd send a letter to the two of them, demanding that they come straight the hell home." As you scoffed, I quietly sat beside you on the bed. "I know, she really said that word."

I listened in disbelief, recalling how Ba had informed me right after we stepped on the plane that we might never see my mother again. During the flight, he had refused to console me, ignoring my sobs and the dirty looks from the other passengers.

"Anyway, it didn't take me five years to figure out the truth. But by then, I'd put in the work, gotten the grades and a rep for being smart." You pointed at your binder, at the random atomic diagrams in your notes. "I know it's stupid, but when it comes to school, I don't want any regrets about not studying. Because that was maybe the one good thing they left me. A reason to keep trying." You shook your head gently. "Even if none of it was real. You feel me?"

I nodded quietly. All of a sudden, I felt your head on my chest. Slowly, I returned your embrace, ignoring the odd sensations in my stomach.

"Thanks for listening," you said. "You've been a real brother."

Still nodding, I mumbled nonsense beneath my breath, unable to respond to your confession with anything meaningful.

See, brother, I wanted to tell you secrets too. Instead, I pretended that I had nothing to say, too afraid at that moment to offer you any comfort or solace. Even though by then, you were already the most important person in my life.

HARVARD. STANFORD. MIT. PRINCETON.

Can you believe that none of them survived the War? When you think about it, the new version of the Gaokao isn't too different from those old pen-and-paper tests; it had always been a marathon of sorts. Still, all that studying we did, all the facts we shoved into our brains—doesn't it strike you now as ironic? That because Qin students can directly download knowledge into their Mindbanks, it would make all our years of cramming worthless?

The Gaokao had to change to be fair for everyone, the Party said.

I'm not complaining; I mean, I wouldn't have scored well on the old exams. I just find it funny that the main criterion they use to evaluate us now is how far we can push ourselves to ignore pain. They want us to run that virtual race until our legs can't move, then they want us to crawl. To keep pushing, past the Swamp, the Desert, the Sea, all the way to their best simulacrum of the Promised Land.

Crawl on. And don't waste any time looking back.

IT TOOK ME AGES TO MAKE IT THROUGH THE SWAMP. SOMETIMES, I pushed forward with my one leg when the ground sloped downward, or when there was some rock I could use as leverage. But mostly I relied on my avatar's arms. I learned to keep my elbows out, to dig my fingers into the dirt. I did my best to ignore the dead sticks and stones slicing my skin.

To give myself strength, I rambled to myself:

This isn't your real body, remember? Cuts can't get infected here. This Swamp can't go on forever. If you crawl far enough, maybe you can score a job in the African Autonomous Economic Zone, somewhere your status as a Qin-American traitor won't matter.

Maybe you could take your father there. Wouldn't that be incredible? If you could bring him to a real land of milk and honey?

I talked to distract myself from the pain. Even when my shoulders were on fire, when I got so tired that I let my avatar fall smack into the mud, I never stopped the internal monologue.

The only time that noise in my head fell silent was when I thought of you. As I crawled through the Swamp, I couldn't help but wonder where you were. Was it someplace where you didn't need to take the Gaokao? Somewhere beautiful, where those new legions of Red Guards can't find you and throw you in a camp, like they did to Ba?

Where did you go? And why did you leave us behind?

I REACHED THE DESERT.

I wish I could say that the marathon got easier after the Swamp. But after I crawled past the final stretch of mud, the land transformed into a horizon of sand dunes. As soon as I crossed the invisible line in the simulation, the temperature swelled to scorching levels.

From a distance, I spotted two slabs of wood sticking out from a dune underneath the blazing sun. Were they meant for me? Could I use them as crutches? It took my last reserves of energy to reach the wood; to my relief, the planks were just tall enough to bear my weight when I slung my arms over them. My throat was so parched that I could barely croak out my gratitude to the heavens.

I began to imagine my avatar melting; I worried that I would pass out, wake up, and discover that I'd somehow quit the Gaokao.

What would happen if I fainted in the simulation? I don't know. It was only pain that kept me awake and stumbling across the hot sand. Pain that lit up my arm whenever I tripped over my makeshift crutches and fell. Pain that coursed through my spine, filling my chest with every exhale of my avatar lungs.

Still, the worst pain came from remembering where Ba was. He sacrificed everything he had in Qin to give me a better life. How could I forgive myself if I didn't do my best in this Gaokao? Even if I never had any real shot of winning academic awards or getting into famous colleges—maybe I could make him proud now.

Even if I wasn't ever going to be like you.

THREE WEEKS BEFORE I TURNED SIXTEEN, I FINALLY ACCEPTED the truth.

It happened on a warm Sunday. Over the previous week, I'd sent you a hundred texts: **Fuck, where'd you go, man?** I tried reaching you on every app. I made Ba drive me to your house to ring the doorbell, then I tried calling your aunt's phone. But when neither of you showed to church, I had no choice but to acknowledge that you were gone.

Service was already over that day. The pews were emptying when I leapt onto the stage near the pulpit. "Reverend Wilson," I yelled, striding toward the altar and blocking his path to the stairs. Never in my life had I spoken to him with that tone. "Did he see you before they left?"

The old man stared at me, a sad smile tugging at the corners of his lips.

"Please. Tell me the truth," I said. "Did he ask for your blessing? Where did they run to? Canada? Mexico?"

The old man's face reddened. Perhaps he was cursed with the inability to lie. Or maybe he had taken one sip too many from his flask.

As the spiteful thought crossed my mind, I felt a stab of guilt that I knew little about the Reverend beyond his time hustling in New York.

For months, I had held my tongue during his sermons about how God would protect us from our enemies, even after Qin had conquered most of its island neighbors while encountering minimal resistance from the West.

You were the only one I confided my fears in, besides my father.

"What the hell has Reverend Wilson been going on about? It's only a matter of time before Qin attacks us too right?" I recall venting at the beginning of the War. "Can't he choose a relevant passage for once? Shouldn't we be planning for the worst?"

I can't remember where we had that conversation. All I can see now is you shaking your head, refusing to engage. I was an idiot to think that you were just being avoidant, too afraid to confront the reality of the coming War, like so many others. Part of me worried that you might have been feeling awkward about my ethnicity, given the wave of anti-Qin sentiments in America at the time. Never in my wildest dreams did I imagine that you might leave without a word. Without any hint that you ever considered asking Ba and me to join you.

By now, members of the congregation were coming toward the pulpit, drawn by the commotion. It didn't matter; I had only minutes before my father returned from the bathroom.

"Do you really think they'll now be safe from the War? How could you let them go? When you preach all day long about keeping faith?" Some of my spittle landed on the Reverend's face accidentally, but I refused to stop. "Aren't you tired of lying? For once, why can't you admit that everything you preach is bullshit!"

The shock on the old man's face nearly took me out of my rage. But before I could yell another word, I felt a pressure on my elbow, jerking me backward. I shook myself free, but a moment later there was another pull, so strong that I nearly toppled off the stage.

Stumbling, I lifted my arms to regain my balance, bracing my hands against the platform. Then I looked up and saw the culprit.

It was Ba.

"Time to go," he said. Apologizing to the Reverend, my father dragged me down the stairs. Shaking him off for a second time, I stormed out before he could lay another hand on me.

In the car, Ba warned that the next time I used that language in church, he'd slap me.

"This isn't Qin!" I yelled, "If you want to hit me, you should've stayed there! Or left me behind with Ma!"

Eyes still trained to the road, my father drove past the ramp for the freeway.

"Hey, where are you doing?" I asked. Suddenly, he swerved and slammed on the brakes; only the seatbelt prevented my body from launching through the windshield. Shutting off the engine, my father turned away, as if trying to avoid meeting my eyes.

"Did you know too?" I asked. "Am I the only one he didn't tell?"

For a while, all I heard were his shallow breaths. Then Ba began to recite a prayer. "Lord, Praise to You that You will not desert me. Father, help me keep faith." To my surprise, not a word was off. "You will not forsake me. Because You are with me."

He stuck his key back into the ignition but did not turn it.

Finally, he spoke, "Of course not." His voice was soft. "Yes, I admire your friend, but you are my son. You are reason why I leave your Ma and our country."

At last, my father started up the engine.

"I have not one regret," he said. "I have not one regret about you, my son."

For the rest of the drive, we sat in silence. I stared ahead, too frightened to turn toward my father and see traces of vulnerability on his face. When we reached our bungalow, he bolted from the car before I could unbuckle my seatbelt.

Several times during the ride, I couldn't help but glance at the rearview mirror, to check whether you were sitting behind us. Of course, all I saw were the empty polyester seats, scratched and covered in dust. The truth is that, even then, I understood that you were only trying to protect us, not wanting to leave any evidence to suggest that Ba and I might have been complicit in your escape, knowledge that might have placed us in harm's way.

Still, no matter how much I rationalized your decision, I could not forgive you.

You were gone. But as I sat in the car, baking in the sun as our front door swung in the wind, I took solace in the fact that I wasn't truly alone. Not when Ba and I still had each other.

FORTY YEARS.

How many times did the Reverend preach about Moses wandering the wilderness with his flock before guiding them to the Promised Land? How many times did you have to wake me when the old man started again about Exodus?

The Desert began to feel like a mirage. The thirst made my ears buzz. I limped along feeling sorry for myself, as if I'd already followed the prophet for decades. As I pulled my body across the dunes, I recalled our trips to the swimming pool. All the times we snuck into the YMCA, too cheap and poor to pay the fees. Then after our swims, when we tried to outlast every white boy who walked into the sauna to prove that we were tougher. As delirium started to kick in, you finally appeared in my mind's eye.

It was as if we were sharing a dream. I began reminiscing about our adventures, talking to you as if you were next to me on the sand: *Did you know that before the YMCA, I never heard that joke about Black kids not knowing how to swim?*

You chuckled. *Damn straight, you were so scared of the water. Made it more fun to teach you.* In my imagination, your face was strangely clean-shaven.

Scared? Above your blue swimming trunks, I saw your abs ripple with every breath. *Well, maybe. Anyway, remember that time we found ourselves alone in the sauna? When I stood up from the heat, so ready to run to the showers—*

I was like: Wait, out of here already? Oh, or you mean when I walked up to those coals . . .

Yeah! One, two, three, you counted—then you made them hiss! It was my turn to laugh. *Of course I joined you up there, standing and pulling down my pants . . . Man, we ran so fast to the change room after, oh Lord—*

We laughed hysterically in my fantasy until I fell silent.

You know—that was my first time seeing anybody's, not even my Ba's . . . I trailed off when you began to nod.

Me too, brother. Me too.

BROTHER. HOW MANY TIMES DID YOU USE THAT WORD WITH ME?

So what if we acted like idiots sometimes? We were fools abandoned by our mothers, who studied too much and played around at church. But we were fools together.

If you have kids one day, how will you tell them our story? Not just the swimming. Will you describe the taste of my father's salted fish and chicken rice? The time you called me frantically when your aunt's forehead was burning up, and we came over to help? Do you remember who sat on the blue plastic seat beside you at the hospital while we waited for the doctors? As my father endlessly circled the block because the parking lot was full?

Brother. That wasn't just a word to me.

Will you make your betrayal seem like some impossible choice? I get it. It's easy to rewrite history when there's nobody around to challenge your version of the past. Reverend Wilson never mentioned this in his sermons, but I can't imagine that the Exodus was inspiring for the Egyptians who had to endure the Ten Plagues.

Imagine the Nile overflowing with blood. The blue skies swarming with locusts, darkness covering the capital for three days. Imagine if your firstborn died in the name of a god that you didn't believe in so that He might demonstrate His infinite might. Wouldn't that make you furious too?

Deep down, I understood. Why you left. Nobody could guarantee that the Party wouldn't send you to reeducation. Although my family had betrayed Qin with our emigration, the choice to leave had not been mine. If the worst came to pass, my father hoped that the color of my skin might protect me. Still, I could not stem my anger. Because if you weren't coming back, what was the point of forgiveness?

Nevertheless, as I wandered across the Desert, I missed you.

THE SEA. I HAD ALWAYS IMAGINED IT TO BE AN INFINITE BLUE vista, melding into the heavens. As I hobbled through the Desert on my crutches, I began to hear the faint collisions of waves against a shore. There wasn't a wisp of a cloud above, no rain or water in sight. The sky was so stunning that I was reminded again this place couldn't be real.

Had I imagined the sounds? All around me there was only sand.

I almost collapsed in despair onto a dune. For the first time, I lifted one of my crutches to the sky and whispered a prayer to the Party. To help me survive, in case any Censors were listening in: *Make this Desert end.*

Please.

I will never know for certain if anyone was paying attention. But a dozen steps later, all the sand was gone. The Desert was over. I found myself at the edge of a cliff, staring at a precipitous drop to a line of black rocks being beaten by the water.

Relief and fear washed over me. How was I going to reach those waves? Was there a winding path down I'd missed? Or was I simply supposed to leap from the cliff? I leaned against my crutches and watched the Sea rage beneath my lone leg, a furious reflection of the blue above. As the scent of salt reached my nostrils, I forgot the pain in my body.

What if they wanted me to pray again?

Blasphemy. Yet I had paid homage to the Party and no bolt of lightning had struck me. Perhaps God's eye did not see into this simulation. If I didn't want to live the rest of my life as a traitor's son, if I wanted to see my father again, did I have any other choice?

Dear Party. It was time for me to accept another religion. Why couldn't I just be proud of being Qin? I was born there. I shared their skin. Slowly I dropped one crutch. Balancing on my remaining sliver of wood, I stood precariously. The only way to survive was to abandon the old ways. How else could I make it to the Promised Land, whatever that meant in this simulation?

Forty years. Let this Gaokao serve as my penance. Let me be done.

Dear Party. Save me.

With every word, I couldn't help but wonder whether you and Ba would forgive me. For forty years, Moses had wandered. How many hours had we spent in those pews? How many songs had we sung in praise of Him? I imagined Ba trying to stop me from committing this sin, just as he had on the day I confronted the Reverend.

I imagined yelling at him: *Admit it, the only reason we walked inside the church on our first day was because you wanted to get me into Catholic school! You didn't even know there were so many denominations of Christianity!*

I saw Ba's face crumple, the same way it did when the Red Guards arrived at our home and charged him for violating the Homeland Loyalty Act.

"Was he the one who made you abandon Qin?" the Guards demanded as they pressured me to renounce my father. Over and over, they repeated their questions until one of them grabbed my hand and forcibly aimed it in Ba's direction. At that moment, I could hear my voice crying out as if from a distance, as tears ran down my father's cheeks . . . Or had the tears been on my face? Unable to bear my memories any longer, I flung my avatar over the cliff into the raging Sea—

Your lips. Your beautiful face appeared in my mind's eye.

I should have died instantly. But the Gaokao refused to end the simulation, refused to let me off so lightly. The Party wanted me to recognize their control, to never forget their power.

As the waves crushed my virtual windpipe, I saw you. Not your face in the final days before you abandoned me, but when I first saw you dressed in white, sitting in the pews that Sunday morning.

Brother, I began to drown.

As my lungs filled with saltwater, I must have screamed a thousand times to be saved. But in my head, all I saw was your loving smile, and the gentle face of God commanding me to forgive.

I HAD TOO MUCH TO DREAM

Last night, your ghost slipped into my room.
I reached for your shadow, memories of us.

It's one of the songs you taught me, she said. Don't you remember?

White mountains loomed in the distance, two streaks of clouds
hanging frozen above them. Giant red cedars stood stubbornly against
the wind, oblivious that their species was on the brink of extinction.
It must have hurt her to stare at the trees, knowing their fate.

Her voice was barely perceptible over the thrum of planes overhead. He remembered bringing her to these woods during one of
their first dates and being so embarrassed that he hadn't scouted
the area in advance for noise pollution. She had forgiven him so
effortlessly that it only made him fall for her harder. Two red birds
swooped from the thick of nearby trees and darted toward the
mountains. He watched their wings transform into a blur of white
as they soared and became small, then smaller yet.

He refused to ask her to hum the tune again to help him iden-
tify the song. Instead, they sat quietly on a knoll, beside her yellow
suitcase, staring ahead.

Where are you flying again? he asked.

Say again?

Again. Again. Ha.

Er, is that supposed to be funny?

I asked where you were flying. Please. Tell me the truth.

She shook her head wearily. Her chin was sharper than he re-membered. He wished that he had gotten her to eat more, sleep more over the last few months. As strands of her hair began to flut-ter in the wind, the tattoo of the eucalyptus leaf on her neck came into relief.

How much time had passed since she had gotten the ink? There was so much she had hidden from him, although the leaf had not been one of her secrets.

It's safer for you not to know, she answered. You promised not to ask.

Gritting his teeth, he stood from the knoll and murmured that he did not want her to miss her precious flight. He stared at her suit-case, quietly scrutinizing the luggage tag for any hint of a destina-tion. Other than her name and phone number, the slip had nothing else on it. She had not even written their address, which they had shared for the past three years.

One week, she said. Or you'll know.

She stood too. Suddenly, she wrapped her arms around him, resting her head against his shoulder. How had she known that he did not want to see her face? Her arms felt so thin. He shivered be-fore pulling back.

Sure, he said. Whatever you want.

He picked up her suitcase from the grass. Walking toward the parking lot, he could not help but glance back at their shadows. It had been silly, he thought, to have brought her here, hoping that she might reconsider the flight after her bag was already packed. When they reached the car, he hesitated, not wanting to confront the mess of gear in the trunk: the unopened tent, hiking poles, flashlights. Was there time to return any of it? The last thing he needed was a reminder of the camping trip that he had planned to surprise her with later in the summer.

Get in, he said.

They did not speak again as they drove through the woods to

the freeway, then the airport. When they arrived, he remained inside the car. As he watched her drag the suitcase through the automatic doors, he felt a wave of shame for not getting out to help.

He ran his hands through his hair in frustration and rubbed his temples. As if any of that might clear the noise in his mind.

SHE WAS RIGHT. ONE WEEK LATER, HE SAW HER PALE FACE ON television.

TWELVE ACTIVISTS "DISAPPEARED" FROM
BANGKOK SUMMIT—

The first time the headline flashed across the screen, he nearly collapsed onto the cold office floor. Gathering himself just enough to reach the bathroom, he promptly emptied his stomach into the toilet bowl. When one of his colleagues asked what was wrong, he reflexively blamed food poisoning, then beelined toward the door. After all, she had made him promise that he would never expose her activism to anyone.

If anything goes wrong, especially if things go wrong, she told him. You have to swear that you won't get involved and risk your safety too.

The conviction in her eyes had scared him. If he wanted her in his life, he did not feel like he could refuse her in that moment, even if he would regret it later.

STILL MISSING: THE TWELVE RUMORED TO
FACE EXTRADITION—

The words were everywhere. He read them on the ticker floating across the giant screen in the cafeteria, the newsletter sent daily to his email, even the smartphones of his colleagues on their shuttle bus to work. One national paper dedicated an entire episode of their popular podcast to the activists' kidnapping, likely by the authoritarian regime the group had been protesting against. He had immediately unsubscribed from the podcast upon seeing the title of the episode, but there was no escape from the ubiquity of technology.

ACTIVISTS CHARGED UNDER NEW SECURITY LAW—

After a month passed with no news about when any of the organizers might be released, he began to avoid eating in the office cafeteria altogether. One cashier, a man with a bent nose, had a habit of dialing up the television volume during his shift. The news anchors would mangle the activists' names, especially those who had not chosen an English moniker. He would feel a stab in his heart every time he heard her name mispronounced or saw it misspelled on closed captioning. He began excusing himself from the weekly team lunches, blaming his absence on the workload.

THAILAND UNDER SCRUTINY FOR EXTRADITION OF THE TWELVE—

The food at the office was free—one of the many perks of working for the search engine relied on by most of the world. For the past three years, he had always hidden an extra container of food on the ledge beneath his desk to bring home to his girlfriend. He had been careful to avoid any strong smells, often agonizing over what dishes might not survive the commute, all to earn a soft peck on his cheek upon his return.

Now he could order anything from the cafeteria he wanted. Sichuan stir-fry. Zucchini linguine. Chorizo pizza. It did not matter what he scooped onto his plate, since there was an equal chance that he would puke it out later. He would sometimes gorge himself, as if to fill the emptiness he felt inside, despite the burning acid that inevitably bubbled up his throat.

HUMAN RIGHTS LAWYERS DENIED ACCESS
TO IMPRISONED—

In the evenings, he did not disconnect but rather logged on to the search giant's news aggregator to read all the articles he had avoided earlier. Mostly, he would refresh the homepage of that popular newspaper with the podcast: superfluously, incessantly.

What else could he do? She had made him swear to stay away. The weight of his promise hung heavy in their apartment. Even when he played their shared playlists to drown out the unbearable silence at home, he still struggled to breathe.

The warmth of your gaze, the linger of your touch,
Left marks that cannot be erased.

THAT MORNING, HE AWOKE FROM A DREAM THAT MIGHT NOT have been awful. Although he could rarely recall his dreams, for the last four months he had woken up with intense dread in his chest. Thankfully today, his lower back felt slightly less tense than the day before, even as his neck crackled upon turning toward the empty side of their bed.

His alarm had not yet sounded. Not that it mattered; he did not need to rush to join the crowd of tired engineers waiting outside for the search engine's shuttle because he was not planning to go to work today. Another car would pick him up; all he had to do was make himself presentable.

Rolling to his side, he staggered to his feet and stared into the open closet they shared, mostly filled with her clothes. Before she flew off, she had thrown some dirty underwear into the hamper and in her absence, he had washed them for her, haphazardly folding them into a pile atop an empty shelf in the closet.

Presentable, he reminded himself. His eyes swept back and forth between the hangers. One of them held his favorite hoodie, featuring a manically typing squirrel that had become his work team's mascot. His eyes stopped on a gray dress shirt that was not too wrinkled.

What could they expect from him? Tie? Blazer?

Later, in the bathroom, the light flickered. Why had he not changed the bulb, after she had asked him so many times? He clawed at his head in irritation, wishing that his nails scraped against more hair and less scalp. As he waited for the light to steady, he stripped off his T-shirt and stared at his body in the mirror, the stubborn rolls of fat that had only thickened since her disappearance.

Gross, he whispered to himself. Gross.

FIVE YEARS AGO, HE HAD MOVED TO THE CITY TO START HIS JOB at the search engine. She was in her first year of a master's in Asian studies program at a university better known for producing technologists than activists. They connected over a dating app founded by a trio of Korean sisters, back when his hair was full and his profile photo did not require filtering to attract matches. On their first coffee date, he arrived early to find her sitting at one of the long faux-wood communal tables, beside half a dozen yuppies typing on their laptops. She was sipping from her own mug, wearing a cardigan that looked small even on her petite frame. He recalled babbling, regretting some of his questions even as they escaped his lips: Why are you paying tuition to study the history of Asia—*from here*?

She surprised him with her answers.

It is impossible to read the full truth in my country, she explained. In my old school, we cannot even criticize our teacher. Don't we need criticism to improve? To get better?

He told her that his parents had emigrated from her country

too, many years ago. They had always talked about bringing him back to visit their hometown, where they'd met and gotten married, but to earn a stable income, their family had purchased a convenience store. No matter if it was Christmas or New Year's Day, the shop was open. They could never bring themselves to step away, much less enjoy an extended holiday on the other side of the world. When he was still in high school, cancer had claimed them both. They had kept their diagnoses a secret from him, not wanting to distract him from his studies.

He refrained from mentioning that his parents' greatest fear might have been their only child majoring in Asian studies, as he'd once joked to a friend.

Her English had impressed him; her accent was barely detectable for someone who had arrived in the country six months ago. He admired her fearlessness, how she had challenged him on his undergraduate thesis on the merits of globalization. As a news junkie, she would reprimand him on the environmental degradation and increased inequalities that neoliberalism had contributed to, as if those were his fault too.

Why did you want to be a product manager? she asked early in their relationship. Why not work somewhere more meaningful than a search engine?

He liked that she had refused to let him off the hook, until he admitted that after growing up in the back of a convenience store, the salary and prestige of working in tech had been too much for him to turn down. Later, she said that she admired his honesty and patience, how he never seemed to mind repeating himself for her benefit, whether the conversation centered on Ruby on Rails or Miley Cyrus.

On that first date, she wore a yellow scarf around her neck. It was a detail he would remember two years later when his girlfriend wanted to buy an umbrella of the same color to demonstrate solidarity with a protest in her home country.

Before then, she had never attended a political rally.

Why do you need an umbrella? he asked. Don't the protesters over there bring umbrellas to defend themselves against tear gas? You don't need to worry about tear gas here, right?

He reminded her that there were several umbrellas in the closet featuring the search engine's logo. She had recently moved into his apartment—perhaps she didn't know about his stash. But she placed the online order anyway, not breathing a word until he arrived home one evening to find the long cardboard box tipped across his doormat.

The afternoon of the rally, he had decided not to go with her, blaming the gloomy weather. Since he was a child, his parents had reminded him that the desire to escape their country's politics was one of the reasons they had emigrated, forsaking their idealism for the more ordinary desires of making money and pursuing happiness. Wouldn't he be disgracing their memory if he now became politically active? After they had sacrificed so much to leave that behind?

They both knew that the rain was an excuse but he was grateful that she did not give him a hard time. Yet he would come to regret his petty rebellion. Had he attended that city hall protest, perhaps she wouldn't have gotten as close to those activists: Frances, Kennedy, and the rest . . . Maybe he bore some responsibility for her radicalization too: he used to joke about her "do-gooder" nature and tell her to stop complaining whenever she grumbled about another humanitarian injustice she had learned about online. Had he been more empathetic and made her feel heard, maybe she wouldn't have gotten involved with such an extremist group.

Although perhaps her turn to activism had been inevitable, as his friends would tell him.

Your girlfriend is an adult. She's responsible for making her own decisions and living with the consequences, his friend Amanda reminded him. Besides, don't you think it's admirable that she's fighting for human rights?

He would nod along to their lectures, especially the ones from friends who came from more repressive countries. After all, how could he blame his girlfriend for supporting such worthy causes, even if he was sick of reading her essays on social media? He soon realized that not even his inner circle of friends was sympathetic to his attempts to stop her from organizing rallies. He began to resent their righteousness. If her parents, who still lived in her home country, knew how she was spending her time instead of finishing her degree, they would have been furious. Why else did she never mention her activism during their calls?

It was easy for people outside their relationship to judge him when they did not have to bear the costs themselves. How could one even begin to guess at the consequences of agitating an authoritarian regime? Who knew how many of their spies had snuck into the country, lived among them? Perhaps they had infiltrated their very neighborhood.

Then there were the little things. Was he simply supposed to stomach her being late to every dinner? His colleagues were forever asking to meet her; it embarrassed him to endlessly invent excuses for her absences. He started to worry that his colleagues might think that she wasn't real, that he had made her up. For goodness' sake, she had even missed his charity half-marathon. Although the event successfully raised more than fifty thousand doallars for Syrian refugees, he knew that his colleague Mariam was displeased that he had been unable to rally his own girlfriend to the cause.

Yet he did not want to become that guy. Someone who needed full control, who demanded his woman do only the things he approved of. Even if he was that guy, he did not want to face that scorn, to be the villain in their tragic love story.

WEEKS AFTER THE ARRESTS, THE TWELVE REMAINED AT THE CENter of international news. Famous anchors pored over the activists' backgrounds and interviewed their families, sometimes with the aid of translators. Relatives broke out in tears on-air. He noticed that the parents speaking were invariably those who had long left the region where their children were now imprisoned. In contrast, the families who still lived in the home country had uniformly rejected all media requests. They knew better than to comment.

He tried reaching out to her parents twice by video call, but they did not answer. Maybe they worried that their accounts were being monitored by the government, or that accepting his call might reduce their social credit score. Maybe they simply did not trust him; they had met only once, when they flew over to attend her graduation. Had they even been aware of their daughter's activism? All he remembered of their visit was how loudly they chatted in their local dialect, and how they made her pose endlessly for photos. Her parents had purchased so much paraphernalia from the university bookstore that they had been forced to leave most of it behind to collect dust in the closet, next to her clothes.

Would it kill you to miss one protest? he recalled asking her once. Would it kill you to not translate the next press release about some march around city hall?

My country is burning, she said. I can't watch and do nothing.

Why are you being so dramatic? he asked, even as he regretted raising his voice.

You don't need to come to the protests anymore, she said. If you don't believe in what we're trying to do.

No, I want to come. I want to support you, he said. Only then did he consider that she might not want him there, if he did not also support her cause.

HUMIDITY.

She used to tell him stories about growing up in high temperatures, the summer sweat lingering on her skin so long that her forearms would become inflamed from heat rashes. Studying without air conditioning, getting wet patches on her shirts when she used to walk along the Bund, back when the view across the river featured few skyscrapers. Waiting hours to share a table at the most famous restaurant in Cheng Huang Temple, the line of hungry tourists and locals snaking past the pavilion and onto the nearby stone bridge. When the famous crab-paste soup dumplings arrived, the wrappers were often flecked with bamboo splinters. She described her mother washing her white-and-green uniforms by hand, hanging them on wooden sticks that extended from the balcony to dry beneath the starless night sky. In the morning, she would wear the same uniform to recite texts in class, sometimes filled with Party propaganda.

"I love the trees. I love my mother and father. But do you know what I love most?" She chuckled as she recalled the lines for him. "The Party and our glorious nation!" Of course!

How did you survive sitting through that? he asked. You of all people?

Everyone wanted to get high scores in class, she explained, because the best students got to study in the room with the air conditioner.

I can't believe you were that easy to bribe, he said. Maybe one day you can bring me to the temple with the soup dumplings.

Her face lit up. He squeezed her cheeks. She batted away his hands, pretending that she did not want him to touch her, then tickled him beneath his armpits as if they were children.

When did their playfulness end? Try as he might, he could not remember.

BY THE THIRD YEAR OF HER ACTIVISM, HE BEGAN HAVING TERRIBLE thoughts—like hoping that her country would burn to the ground so that his girlfriend would return to his side.

Why can't you pick another issue? he often asked. Aren't the forests burning too? Don't you care about our planet? Or the homeless people downtown? Wealth inequality?

She did care about those issues, she explained. But this was different. It was her home.

I thought I was your home now, he said, pretending not to see the sadness in her eyes.

Her activism had gone too far; he was not even sure it was safe for her to fly back to her country after the local newspaper had published a series of articles about the rallies she'd organized, accompanied by photographs where she had raised her face defiantly to the camera, unmasked.

He wanted to scare some sense into her. But short of reporting her to that authoritarian regime, what could he do?

Would you even care if I broke up with you? Because of the activism, all the risks you're taking? he once yelled at her in anger. Because you never put us first?

Nobody knows my real name, she said in defense. Not like Kennedy—

Kennedy? Kennedy's never going back there! His entire family lives here. Are you really okay with never seeing your parents again?

That was the last thing he said before she walked away in cold fury.

He started to notice new apps on her phone, encrypted messaging platforms she used to chat with her fellow organizers. Every time he saw the notifications pop up, he felt a strong urge to grab her phone and delete the apps. But what was the point when she could simply tap and redownload?

During their arguments, the same defiant expression that had been plastered in the papers would flash across her face. Nobody knows my real name, she would remind him.

I'm a small fry, she added sometimes.

Once, they began laughing because, of all her online pseudonyms, she was best known as WHITEWHALE. He tried to compose himself, saying that there was nothing funny about the risks she was taking, nothing funny at all. Then he wrapped his arms around her, smiling as they resumed their cycle of fighting, then making up. Over and over again.

WHEN SHE FIRST BEGAN TO TRAVEL FOR HER ACTIVISM, SHE TOLD him everything: where she was flying, what websites would be live-streaming the rallies. But when her group of misfits began lobbying foreign governments, the leadership implemented a new policy of keeping their itineraries secret. She had refused to break the rules, not even for him.

The less you know, the safer we'll all be, she said.

Who came up with this? Kennedy?

He pictured Tony Leung or some other dashing actor in a three-piece suit, even as he knew that the protesters were rarely well dressed. More often, he saw her friends wearing sweaty T-shirts, dragging dirty speakers along the road and herding protesters away from police while attempting not to drop their microphones and crumpled flags.

What do you have against Kennedy?

He did not answer. Instead, he canceled the subsidiary credit card that he had given her to book flights and collect loyalty points. By then, she had stopped receiving her graduate stipend, having missed too many classes to successfully convert her master's degree into a PhD.

He had expected her to get mad, to call him immature. It will be worth it in the end, he thought. She'll forgive me.

But he had miscalculated. He had underestimated her, or rather the plethora of human rights organizations and campaigns willing to fund her. Now he could not even log into their joint frequent-flyer account to see where she was traveling.

One week, she promised him. I'll try to keep the trips to under a week.

What do you even do on these trips? he asked.

When she refused to answer, he was stunned to find himself no longer surprised by her silence. I'll be safe, she said. Isn't that enough?

No, he almost said. Not even close.

Yet, even as he lectured her, he secretly understood her perspective—for he too had begun following the politics in her country. Her fire, albeit metaphorical, had transformed into something real to him as well. In a far-flung region, minorities were being rounded up into camps. Certain media outlets had begun to warn of genocide; yet few wealthy nations seemed to care. The more people rounded up for "re-education," the less he could blame her for getting angry. But then what could her small protests achieve? Her ragtag group of organizers were dreamers, drunk on their impossible fantasies of revolution.

What dreams could be worth such risks?

For such minuscule odds of change, he hated how she prioritized her activism over their relationship, how unequivocal it was that she loved her cause more than him.

When the morning crept in, you dissolved,
Away with the break of dawn.

AS THE SUN ROSE OVER THE CLOUDS, THE APARTMENT BEGAN TO warm. He readied himself to leave. Likely they already knew his address, but he had felt more comfortable meeting in public, even if it meant a steep climb to the nearby bodega.

At the top of the hill, he noticed a lone red sedan parked by the store. An Asian man with a chubby face leaned against the hood, smoking something sweet. When their eyes met, the man waved wildly, nearly knocking off his glasses. The logo of a private college took up most of the space on his sweater. Taking off his crimson baseball cap, he revealed an immense bald spot.

Christ. Was that Kennedy?

The dearth of charisma was stunning. He looked nothing like Tony Leung. If only she had shared a photo; for so long, he had worried whether there was something going on between them. Despite the shame, he had considered snooping on her phone, even though he was aware that her messaging app periodically deleted all encrypted conversations.

Smiling, Kennedy extended his free hand. The shop was still closed, the steel gate lowered to the ground.

One of the red sedan's side mirrors was cracked. Why had he not gotten the glass replaced? Was he that lazy?

I think we met once before at a rally, Kennedy said. Not that you would remember. I'm so glad that you reached out to us.

The tone of his voice was surprisingly warm.

The rest of our team will meet us at the studio. In case you were wondering where everyone else was, the activist said. Most of them don't own cars, to tell the truth.

He nodded. Tapping his foot against the asphalt, he gestured to Kennedy that he was ready to go. But the activist did not move, savoring another puff of smoke from his joint instead.

What was the guy up to?

He shivered in his gray shirt, trying to telegraph his discomfort without making things too awkward. Already, he regretted not wearing his typing-squirrel hoodie.

I want to let you know that it's brave, what you're doing, Kennedy said. Not that your email was a surprise. Amber was always talking about you.

A wave of guilt coursed through him. No, it was impossible. That wasn't even his girlfriend's name, just another pseudonym that she used in the community. Still, he couldn't resist asking more.

Really? What did she say?

All good things. I'm sure she would've been proud.

Anger rose in his chest, displacing the guilt as he listened to Kennedy's use of the past tense. He stared at the ground around the bodega, littered with cigarette butts. He refused to believe that his name had come up during her activism. She wouldn't have held him in mind; she probably did not even remember that she had once written down the group's private email to appease him. It happened so long ago, before she made him promise to stay away. The past tense made everything he was about to do seem futile.

He scowled.

Why couldn't you have gone there instead of her? He caught the words in his head just in time. Kennedy had been born in this country too. No different from him.

What was she like with you guys? he asked instead. Did you know her? Like, for real?

The activist lowered his joint. Sure, I think. Why?

I want to understand if she really knew the risks. When she flew over there.

Under the morning light, Kennedy's teeth revealed a yellow tint as his mouth opened and closed. A frown appeared on the activist's face, casting silhouettes across his cheeks.

You know that none of us could have predicted what happened, right?

Yes, of course . . .

It was Thailand. Not North Korea. Some of them were even treating it like a vacation, a chance to eat good curry and visit the beaches.

He shouldn't have asked: this man was one of the dreamers. The thought of treating a human-rights conference as a holiday made him slightly nauseous . . .

Not her though. Amber was the exception. She wanted to skip it.

What?

Yeah. Did she not say anything?

He swallowed, then took a deep breath. No. I assumed that she wanted to go on every trip. She sounded so certain, so confident.

Kennedy scoffed in disbelief.

Nah, she was always the pragmatic one. We had to drag her along, especially when she believed that our funds could've been better spent elsewhere. She was just so compelling onstage, full of energy. After all, unlike most of us, she'd grown up there.

Kennedy's eyes were shining. The activist adjusted his glasses and laughed awkwardly.

I'm sorry. I can't believe that this is how we're meeting and now I'm running my mouth. We should get going.

Kennedy opened the front passenger door. The seat was occupied by a duffel bag bursting with wrinkled collared shirts and a green Dartmouth College sweatshirt. Shrugging apologetically, the activist squeezed inside and clumsily shoved the bag to the back.

Sorry, my law school friend is moving to Shanghai to take care of his sick parents, so I need to drop off some of his things at the Salvation Army, he said. The timing was a real shame. My friend just started his own practice.

Kennedy sighed. We should have more than enough time for the detour. Unless you need to practice your speech with me? No? Are you sure?

He shook his head, patting his pocket to feel the folded pages tucked inside. Nothing he had written down was revolutionary. It was merely a statement for the cameras, a declaration that he was going to keep making noise until she and her fellow activists were freed. Not that he expected the statement to accomplish anything. Plenty of spouses had dedicated their lives to freeing their imprisoned partners; down the road, most of them became exhausted after organizing marches and collecting foreign human-rights awards in absentia. But this way, he would have at least risked something for her. Wasn't that worth something?

Great, the studio's only a few miles away, Kennedy said. We can rush the video for release this morning. It'll be their evening, so we can get a ton of views before it gets blocked.

A gust of wind blew the joint from his hand down the hill.

Oh, God. Sorry, I'm not a litterbug, believe me . . .

The guilt on Kennedy's face looked genuine. As they stood above a graveyard of cigarettes, he struggled not to snicker.

Clearly you're on the verge of breaking bad, Kennedy.

He watched the activist reach for his cap and rub his bald spot.

Christ. You even brought along clothes to drop off at the Salvation Army. Roll up another, take a toke. Seriously. Do you think I give a shit about litter?

He stared down the hill, beyond the red sedan. He suddenly imagined the flame flickering at the end of Kennedy's joint, then dying in the wind in a blur of ash white. He recalled the line his girlfriend used to repeat whenever she had a smoke.

I mean, the world's already burning. Right?

IN THE CAR, HE STARED AT THE SUN AS IT ROSE FARTHER ABOVE THE skyline. He peered out the passenger window as Kennedy drove south, in the direction of her former college. Many of the taller buildings had been constructed over the past few years to accommodate the hiring frenzy by tech companies. Several stores run by Hispanic families—the taco stalls, thrift shops, and bodegas—had already disappeared. He regretted that he had never been able to show his parents around. Then for the first time, he was glad they were dead. His parents would never have approved of him falling in love with someone like her, certainly not anyone with as dangerous a flaw as selflessness.

The tattoo parlor that had inked her years ago with the eucalyptus leaf had fallen victim to the city's gentrification too. He had learned of its fate last week after taking the train there out of nostalgia. It had been replaced by a bubble tea shop.

Wow. Is that tattoo permanent?

He remembered the anxiety in his stomach when he asked her, after she pushed aside her dark hair to reveal the leaf on her neck for the first time. She had gotten it one afternoon when he was away attending an employee town hall at the search engine campus. He had brought fish tacos home that night from the cafeteria.

I mean, how can you be sure that's the tattoo you want?

He recalled her beautiful face beaming with pride. Because you're my koala, she said. Her gentle voice echoed in the walls of his memory.

Because you're my koala, and I'm your tree.

In the sedan, he began humming.

I had too much to dream last night. Bring back the dark, or leave me with your light . . .

As they entered a graffitied tunnel, he pretended not to hear Kennedy ask for the song's name. If she were next to him now, would she be proud of him for speaking up, even if that meant breaking his promise? Closing his eyes, he imagined her lips moving softly to the music, mouthing each English word with a weary smile, as if she had long accepted all that was to come.

THE REINCARNATION

— Go on, tell her. It's safe.

Many moons ago, beneath the ashes of a forbidden store, my brother and I discovered a book of poems peeking out from the rubble.

I recall that the cover was dark like midnight, a different shade from the crimson parchments on Ba's shelf. We were children, but our Mindbanks must have been installed. Otherwise, I would certainly not remember the verses as well as I do.

Each poem rang out in my mind as if it were a song. The first poem was titled "Soot," like the black powder staining its pages. My brother would crawl into my bed and repeat each verse in a lilting, playful voice.

The poem ended like this:

with the gentleness
of someone delivering tragic news to a child.

⊐ Breathe. Admire the light that emanates from her skin. Remember that you no longer possess eyelids, nothing to shield you from the world. Fold your arms across your chest, as if the gesture might protect your mechanical heart: tick, tick, ticking like a clock.

The Angel appears in your windowless cell every day, a smiling hologram asking for your stories and wanting to talk about the poems. Dark, luscious hair encircles her face, a slender nose and thick lips. She is beautiful. Her glowing skin, the light that radiates from the center of her body, is nearly enough to make you forget about her wings, perfect in their symmetry.

Little Guo, she calls. The white feathers along her back flutter in unison when she giggles. Except it is not the microphone embedded in your carbon-composite body that registers her voice but rather your consciousness. After all, the Angel is only here via connection to your Mindbank. She has never visited in the flesh.

Look around. You are surrounded by four walls, white expanses of reinforced steel that not even your powerful new arms can break. Every day the Angel appears to offer you company in this observation room, where you must stay until she approves your reentry into Qin society. She encourages you to pass the time between her visits with Memory Epics, reexperiencing the stories of other citizens downloaded to your Mindbank.

You are among the first to undergo the process of Reincarnation, the Angel says. *They are keeping you to monitor your inherited memories for errors. For your own well-being.*

Is this truly Reincarnation? What part of this mechanical body can you call your own? Stare at your new hands built from carbon-composite fibers, lighter and stronger than any material you touched during your first life. Touch your new forehead, utterly devoid of hair.

Is what the Angel says true? Are you the same person you were before your death?

Naturally, you expected to become ash, skin and bones melted by a furnace and laid to rest in a porcelain jar. Never did you expect the data from your Mindbank to be preserved, your memories stored for the day that Qin technology advanced enough to return your consciousness to the living.

What is it that you really want to know, Angel?

The Angel smiles. She patiently accepts your every emotion without a ripple of discontentment on her exquisite face.

Everything, she says. *Tell me about your family, Little Guo. And the poems.*

三 *We were twins. Four delicate hands, four identical feet. Though our family owned an entire floor of the Tower, my brother and I shared a room. Because we had each other, we grew up strangers to loneliness.*

At night, we read beneath our covers. Often the poems surprised us, like "Milk," which sung about curves rather than the white fluids that once spewed from the udders of animals:

A curve is a straight line broken at all its points so much
of being alive is breaking

Our Qin stomachs never held much tolerance for the delicacies of the American-white, so neither of us could quite understand what invisible relationship existed between milk and curves. Nevertheless, we kept faith in the poet as we wondered about his true origins.

Was Kaveh Akbar his real name, or some invented moniker to shield him from the Red Guards? Neither of us knew, nor did we dare ask Ba.

It was because of the poet's name that we came to believe the book was a translation, published in the Fourth World. We surmised that the demonic figure on the smoke-stained cover was a citizen from the Desert Colonies, that the fabric over its face was not meant to strike fear but rather reveal secrets from its culture, likely sad and desolate like the ending lines of "Milk":

I cannot be trusted to return
paradise lies
at the feet of mothers I will believe you when you tell me your dreams

四 Tell the Angel that your mother perished bringing you two into the world. How your Ba never took another wife afterward.

Sorry, Little Guo. I had no choice but to ask.

Was this the first time you mentioned your mother to the Angel?

Repetitions are essential for quality control, she explains. *Sometimes I need you to tell me twice. I hope that is not too much trouble.*

Tell her that she should stay with you longer then. Her skin flickers. Enjoy the soft flap of her immaculate wings. Relax your arms. Don't they almost feel lighter when you smile?

Do you find it worrisome that you were attracted to the poet's verses? Given his foreign origins?

Shake your head and ask her not to judge so harshly. After all, you were children, with no mother to teach you patriotism. The Angel nods.

Relax, you tell yourself. You've already passed away once. These conversations cannot end with a worse fate. Even if you have yet to earn your freedom, isn't this better than oblivion?

五 *He was born eight minutes before me, so I called him Da Ge.*

Da Ge had a kind heart. Although he was our father's preferred son, Da Ge still sought to win Ba's praise at every opportunity, especially at our dinners. To keep the peace, I often let him win our arguments. What I struggled more to ignore were my father's fleeting glances from across the table, his dark eyes sometimes overflowing with recrimination, as if to say that although my mother had birthed him two children, only one was worthy of his blood.

Naturally, I came to prefer home when Ba was away, traveling to conduct business negotiations unresolvable via Mindbank. When it was just us brothers, we delighted in experiencing new Memory Epics. Often, we reread Akbar's mellifluous poems late into the night.

We continued in this way until our 140th moon, when I found myself struggling with a verse in "Learning to Pray." I began to recite the poem for my brother:

I hardly knew anything yet—
not the boiling point of water
or the capital of Iran,
not the five pillars of Islam
or the Verse of the Sword.

When I finished, I handed him the physical book so he could read the passage himself. To my surprise, Da Ge returned the pages almost as soon as he touched them, furrowing his brow.

"Oh, stop trying to teach me a lesson," I said, assuming that he was about to criticize me for not thinking hard enough to arrive at the answer myself. "This is our thing. We always discuss Akbar's poems together."

Only after prodding did Da Ge explain. Quietly, he pointed out many offenses in the passage I had quoted. For instance, besides listing several illicit religions, Akbar had failed to even mention our divine Party, much less conclude that it was the only acceptable faith.

"The Party could nationalize our father's business for this offense," he said, raising his voice. "Promise me you'll never show the book to anyone." I nodded. But my brother was still dissatisfied.

"Swear to me, Guo." He made me repeat my vow over and over. In my dreams, I am still uttering promises to him.

六 Ask her: is my brother alive?

The Angel revealed that your father had passed, but she never mentions Da Ge. Why? Is your brother waiting Outside? If the Qin scientists can bring you back, surely they can also fix . . .

The Angel sighs, folding her beautiful white wings across her chest. *Little Guo, will you be angry if I do not answer?*

Breathe through your frustration.

This is a sensitive topic, that of your brother. I need you to tell me more—

Stand up. Punch the wall. Punch it again, even if its steel won't break. After all, your new hand cannot register pain.

Should I record this sudden violence as a side effect of your Reincarnation?

Glare at her flawless visage. Her eyes shine like the pale ivory of piano keys. Is there even a human behind those eyes, operating the avatar? Did they optimize the Angel's features to seduce you, using viewing data from your past life? From your favorite sexual Memory Epics?

May we return to task, Little Guo? I want to finish this process so that I can approve your reentry into Qin society—

Clench your fists. Why does she keep ignoring your questions?

What is it that you are really trying to learn, Angel? Why don't you just scan my Mindbank? You knew about the poems when we met. So why do you make me recite every verse?

She vanishes. Just like that, the wings and light—gone. Her smile too.

Angel? Where are you?

The thought that she might have disappeared forever makes me punch the wall again. If only I could still feel physical pain to distract from my fears.

Don't leave me alone. Angel? Where have you gone?

七 Here was my brother's favorite poem:

To make life first you need a dying star
This seems important with you so close to
collapsing yourself.

Come back to me, Angel. Have I recited this for you before? Is that why you won't return?

This was the final poem I discussed with him.

Will it be the last one I share with you too?

八 Her glow seems fainter than when she last visited. Check your Mindbank.

Tell me about the night of your Gaokao, the Angel asks. For a moment, you wonder if you can escape her interrogation through humor, perhaps by deprecating yourself for your historical lack of interest in the exam. She follows with another question before you can even try. *Did you not have an important conversation with your father that night?*

Feel your mechanical heart race. How do you not get Ba in trouble? You doubt that all the memories you inherited upon Reincarnation would pass the Censors' scrutiny, especially after another five hundred moons of Party rule . . .

Do not fear, Little Guo. We would never Reincarnate your father just to punish him for sharing memories with his born-again son.

Do not trust her. Keep telling patriotic stories of your brother, tales of his loyalty:

With each passing moon, Da Ge recited fewer poems in my presence. Before long, he refused to even touch the physical book which had been our greatest treasure.

"Hide it. Destroy it. Don't tell anyone. It is a miracle that nobody has discovered this secret beneath our beds," he said. "I have the poems in my Mindbank anyway."

Why did that matter if we could no longer talk about them? From the glint in his eyes, I wondered whether he would even care if I burned the book right there in front of him. In the ensuing silence, I helplessly imagined the distance between our hearts growing.

I still remember the afternoon before the Gaokao when Da Ge sought to remind me of my familial obligations. He was wearing a scholarly robe, more befitting of an Elder than someone our age. "You must prepare for the test, little brother," he told me. "The Party will be watching." I recall shrugging at his words; I had never seen much reason to perform well in the Gaokao. The exam that once tested our knowledge now assessed our mental resilience; there was little one could do to prepare for a virtual marathon. Or so I believed.

"Must I spell it out for you?" he asked.

"Speak plainly," I demanded. "If you still respect me, brother."

"Fine, I do not want you to embarrass our family."

Take a breath. Did she really need you to recite his exact words? Even on your new carbon-composite features, the shame on your face should be evident. She gently places one of her wings on your back, allowing you to feel the texture of every feather through her embrace.

More. The Angel asks you to keep talking.

You are not free from her questions. There is no escape, for she wants to know everything you remember about Ba too.

九 If you lie, will she know? If you omit certain details, would the story still ring true?

Would the Angel punish you? Can you trust her with the whole truth, just once?

十 *The night of my Gaokao, I returned to my Tower exhausted. Although my body did not run the race, my mind had been stumbling across a Swamp for over a week. Unexpectedly, I had performed well and reached the Desert. Secretly, I wondered if I had gone farther than my brother, a fleeting arrogance that haunts me still.*

Go on. Speak. How will you gain your freedom if you do not satisfy her?

Upon my return, I discovered Ba in a Zhongshan tunic, waiting in our living room. There was no food on the table, so he must have sent away the maid. The skin on my back began to crawl when I saw him dressed in such formal attire.

He asked me to join him in the study. Immediately, I inquired about Da Ge, whose Gaokao had been scheduled before mine. My father grimaced, standing in the center of the room.

"Tell me if any of this sounds familiar."

He began to recite:

I'm becoming more a vessel of memories than a person ...
It's a myth that love lives in the heart.

My lips turned cold. In a whisper, I finished the poem:

It lives in the throat.
We push it out when we speak.
When we gasp we take a little for ourselves.

His tone was incredulous.

"Poetry. Written by a foreigner, no less."

十一 The Angel laughs when I tell her that is all that I remember.

Her wings stretch out to cover the entire cell. *I know there is more, Little Guo,* she says. *We've gone through this night before.*

Why does she keep pushing then? *So punish me. Like you did Da Ge—*

She asks for the name of the poem your father recited. In your confusion, the title does not surface in your mind. Pretend that your silence is an act of rebellion, of familial loyalty.

It's touching, she says. *That even after death, you are still trying to protect them.*

Abruptly, her face twists and you are reminded that the Angel is no guardian, no savior of your soul.

No, she cannot force you to recount anything. Not if you refuse to speak.

If you insist, I can finish it for you. The Angel's face relaxes. Her tenor suddenly shifts to match that of your voice. And then you recognize that you have no power here—because she is uttering the very words you would have used to narrate your secret. As if this were all a recording, because you have told this story before.

Her voluptuous lips part. In your voice, she speaks:

十二 *Slowly, I pieced together the horror that had befallen my brother.*

"I was certain that you would've been smarter. Deleted every verse. Gifted the poems away," Ba said. "I never thought that either of you would bring them to the Gaokao, a place where your thoughts could be monitored. Or that during the final stage of the Sea, one of you might recite a poem out of delirium . . ."

I slumped to the floor. When I tried to get up, I realized that my muscles had lost their strength. Then Ba was there, beside me on the ground.

I could not bear to glance up at his face.

"When did you find out?" I asked. "What will the Censors do to him?"

"You boys never met your mother," my father said. "But I promised her that I would look after you."

"You didn't answer me, Ba. When did you know—"

"Of course I knew! I always knew!" Dust rose in the air as I slid backward. My father reached out to grab my arms, so tightly that they became numb.

"Many times, I considered entering your room to burn those pages!" The black cover of Akbar's book curled into ashes in my mind. *"But then I thought, what good would that do?"*

"You boys had tasted the sweetness of poetry." Ba's voice softened. *"As I did when I was your age."*

My breathing faltered. At last, I lifted my eyes to meet his gaze.

"Some nights I stood by your door and listened. The words that you boys chanted were so dangerous, so magnificent. Better than anyone, I understood that if I forbade the poems, their allure would only grow. Just like the novel I once hid under my bed—of a tragic romance between a sickly boy from New Tianjin and a girl from Inner Mongolia."

Tears began to well in my father's eyes. But he did not wipe them. Instead, he bore them in silence, as he had done for our secret. Slowly, he released my arms.

"How do we get Da Ge home, Ba?" I pleaded. "We can't let the Censors keep him. He won't survive their questioning. His Mindbank will be devastated . . ."

My father's tunic creased as he buried his face in his hands.

"I don't know, son. I don't know."

十三 Brush your hands against the cold walls, note how its steel has been reinforced to keep you inside. Try to ignore the glee radiating from the Angel's limpid eyes.

How? Ask her again. *Why do you visit me if you already know everything?*

Memories begin to surface uncontrollably in your Mindbank. The return of Da Ge in a wheelchair, after the Censors removed so many memories that his mind no longer functioned. The countless days you sat beside him in the study as he stared blankly Outside. All the prayers you whispered to the Party to repair his mind.

Your brother had lost his sense of self, his ability to comprehend the present after too much of his past had been taken.

The Angel speaks again in your voice:

Sometimes, I longed for the poetry of Akbar. Then I would hate myself more. If there was one who should have been punished for the transgression of those poems, it was not my brother.

I was the one who pulled the book from the rubble, who first recited those verses.

I was the one who should have been punished.

十四 *Angel, you are making me disappear.*

At last, you understand. It took you so long to arrive at the truth. It is only when she asks you to describe your death that you realize your silence is not due to stubborn resistance.

You can't remember how you died. The memory is gone.

You ask me these questions to check what remains. To ensure that your erasures worked exactly as intended during my Reincarnation.

That is what you meant by quality control.

The Angel smiles. Those lips you once adored glisten, even though there's no other light in the room. It makes sense now, why they allowed you to download the memories of your former transgressions. You won't be allowed to keep them.

Her lips move, but once more it is your voice:

Devastation occurs
whether we're paying attention or not.

Wait for the poem to finish. Or is the entire poem comprised of one verse? What if she is tricking you with lines that were never in the book? But if she cannot be trusted, who else can you believe?

What is left of you if your own memories cannot be relied on?

If you use your carbon-composite arms now to rip out your Mind-bank, will you even remember your act of resistance tomorrow? When the Angel inevitably returns to your side?

Little Guo, the violence in your heart will soon disappear, she says. Upon her command, your mechanical functions begin to shut down. *Rest. You have lived a hard life.*

Wait—

One day, you will awake with only serenity. No more guilt. No more anger or other reasons to resist. Then with the grace of the Party, you will be welcomed home.

How did I die? Can you tell me that? Please!

The Party will gift you a new apartment in a Tower. You will befriend your neighbors, all loyal citizens of Qin. We may never cross paths again. But if we do, you will be grateful to me for helping you remember, as your first friend upon Reincarnation.

You're most welcome, Little Guo. Most welcome, my dear.

十五 Go on, tell her. It's safe. Tell the beautiful Angel what you remember, so that she may soon release you into your second life:

Many moons ago, beneath the ashes of a forbidden store, I discovered a black book peeking out from the rubble. I recall that there was another boy there, who remarked that the cover was darker than the crimson parchments on my father's shelf.

How did he know about Ba? The boy ripped the book from my hands, then ran off into the darkness. Or did I hand it to him? I wish I could remember enough to report him.

We were both children then, so our Mindbanks must not yet have been installed. Still, I cannot let go of the feeling that the book was about twins.

It happened so long ago, Angel. One fleeting memory of being mesmerized, by the soot between my fingers from blackened pages.

So why can't I shake this sense of loss?

FANTASIA

There was never any reason not to believe them.

For a long time, we had watched the dark smog from our homes with anxiety, many of us choosing to avoid the Outside entirely; so when the Party warned that the next flash flood from the polluted clouds might scorch our skin, no one questioned their command to ascend permanently to the Towers and live in seclusion. It was around this time that I married Ming, so when I rode up the Accelerator to our marital apartment, I saw little reason to descend afterward.

The truth is that I cannot recall much from those moons, having dutifully uploaded most of the memories to my Archives at the time to make space for the Party's updates. Still, I remember the argument my husband made via voice to convince me to stop working. His logic had been airtight—my income as a virtual schoolteacher was minimal relative to the respect he would gain in the eyes of his colleagues for shouldering our family expenses, respect that would likely advance his lucrative career as a senior Censor. So as one would expect, I agreed to stop working a job I loved in order to honor my husband, saving my reservations only for my mother.

To my surprise, Ma did not share my concerns. When we connected via Mindbank, she was ecstatic that I might follow in her footsteps and become a housewife. By obeying my husband and performing the duties of a perfect Qin wife, I would also honor our entire family; or so that is how my mother reframed my situation, in a long and impassioned lecture.

"So what if he wishes for you to prioritize his career over your own? Does he not put Nutrilent on the table? Did he not give you a home in the tallest Tower with the latest Accelerator? What more could you dream of?"

In hindsight, I should not have been surprised. Of course Ma did not want to risk losing the allowance I sent home each moon from Ming's salary. Moreover, she was the one who had discovered him on an online marriage market and arranged for us to meet. In her mind, she had done me a great service, especially given how little I had to offer a husband: a few ordinary memories, barely enough to call an inheritance.

"If I had your single eyelids and bitter tongue, your father would never have chosen me!" Ma reminded me. "Be grateful for the experiences we purchased that made you desirable to this fine man. Your education wasn't free!"

When Ming and I first connected via our Mindbanks, I remember being surprised that he had uploaded his own features rather than pay to use the face of some Memory Epic star as his avatar. More shocking were the scars around his mouth, signs that he had survived a mutation of the Chrysanthemum Virus, which devastated our world many moon millennia ago. His family must have been wealthy enough to obtain the cure. Later, I would learn that a large part of their fortune had been wiped out by his father's decision to save him; still, the statistics streaming next to his avatar, namely his vault of memory assets, were enough to make my eyes widen.

"Um, am I rich enough for you?" I blurted, the first words he heard from my avatar's lips. Ming looked stunned, then broke out in laughter. Within ten moons, he would pay for my hand with a dowry so generous that even Ma experienced an unfamiliar sense of pride in her daughter.

WE WERE AT HOME. TIME AND AGAIN, I HAVE REVISITED THAT EVEning in my Mindbank, so the scene remains vivid in my head. It was nightfall. Staring out the floor-to-ceiling windows of our apartment, I pressed my palm against the solar glass, feeling the lingering warmth from the afternoon sunlight. Although the Party never confirmed the health risks, rumors ran rampant that the smog could cause everything from black lung to infertility. As I watched the clouds swirl beneath, I recalled the last time I had been out of the Tower, so fearful of the invisible toxins that suffused the Outside.

Sometimes I wonder if it was only coincidence that I felt such anxieties so close to my husband's announcement, or whether the timing contributed to my shock. Yet, I don't think that there was any way around the strangeness. Because under what circumstances would any sane Qin husband tell his wife that he wanted to leave for the Outside—to go running!

With a straight face, Ming told me he wanted to run Outside, beyond the gates of our Tower. Can you believe it? After he told me, I remember walking away from the window to our bedroom, where I began to fold laundry. Perhaps I had misheard; I refrained from mentioning that he had not even reapplied for my Outside permit after it had expired.

"Why are you upset?" Ming said as he trailed me into the room. I ignored him, trying to focus on my hands as they deftly moved between the garments on our bed. We had recently lost our Fourth World maid and I wanted to remind him of my worth as a homemaker.

"Please, wife. What's troubling you now?"

Arranging his clean robes into an immaculate pile on the bed, I sighed and lifted my eyes. "Shouldn't you know better?" I said wearily. "Did you not hear the news of the Elder who turned mad while Outside? The AI security captured him dancing naked, his skin fully exposed to the pollution."

Ming shook his head. "There are many reasons why citizens suffer from mental illness. There was no evidence in that case that the Outside was to blame."

Before I could argue, my husband raised his palm.

"The Party has already cleaned up the skies," Ming said. "I'm not supposed to say anything, but they will announce the good news soon, I'm sure."

"I don't believe you. If that were true, why would they wait?"

He laughed. "Sometimes I forget that you haven't become as cynical as us Censors. Think carefully—if the news were made public, citizens would start demanding new infrastructure again. Plus, there are still limits to Mindbank surveillance; it's been far easier to monitor Dissident activities when almost no one is Outside."

He dropped his Scroller onto the bed, which quickly disappeared beneath the sea of clothes I had yet to fold. "Look after my Mindbank, dear," he said jokingly, as if I would dare access his backup memories without permission. Ming reached over and squeezed my hand. "I've had a frustrating day and need a change of scenery."

I stared at the scars on his face, stunned. Was this really my husband? Save for essential maintenance, why would anyone want to actively disconnect from their Mindbank? If he suffered an asthma attack while Outside, how would he call for help? Worse, what if a Dissident ambushed him? Or me at home, while he was gone? Perhaps the heat had addled his brain. After all, large swaths of Qin had recently been blanketed by scorching temperatures.

"Do you take pleasure in making your wife worry?" I said, trying a gentle turn of phrase that I had learned from Ma. "What will you do if someone attacks you?"

"Worry? Our complex has the tightest security in the neighborhood." He waved off my concerns. "I'm just so tired of virtual meetings. Every time the Party comes out with new Memory Epic regulations, we have endless debates about how to interpret them." He smiled, shaking his head. "I'm more than just a Censor, you know. Sometimes I want to enjoy other things."

Before I could enquire what madness had taken hold of him, my husband pushed himself up from the bed and began sprinting

toward the door as if he were an antelope from the African Autonomous Economic Zone.

I could not believe my eyes! When I finally accepted that he was
gone, I replayed the memory in my Mindbank of what had trans-
pired. I had heard of Fourth World cults that believed in discon-
necting from our devices, but those groups had disappeared after
the War, after Mindbanks freed us from the One Moment. Not for
a hundred moons had I heard of Qin citizens "running" to improve
their health, and certainly not beyond the gates of their Towers.
Three moons had passed since our last attempt at procreation. If my
husband desired a worthwhile change, why not resume our efforts
in the bedroom to honor the Party instead?

This must be a phase, I told myself. Surely I had no cause to
worry.

But of course, my husband's obsession only grew with each
sweat-drenched shirt tossed into the laundry, until he was spending
over an hour Outside each day. And then even I, a faithful wife who
had never doubted his fidelity, began to question if my husband was
really pounding pavements every night.

AT FIRST, I DID NOT WANT TO MAKE A FUSS. I WAS CONTENT TO
distract myself with Memory Epics I had yet to experience: among
them, the triumphant story of an armless swimmer who sacrificed
for his village's glory, and a cautionary tale about a Qin traitor suffering as an immigrant in former Manhattan, separated from his
wife and son. Yet none of those stories gave any insight into my
troubles. Beyond the fact that my struggles appeared trivial compared to the ones endured by those protagonists, the setting of their
stories seemed otherworldly. Even as I marveled at the beauty of
the sunset upon the Yangtze River, the taste of braised beef noodles
in my mouth—I was reminded that the freedom that our ancestors

enjoyed also brought them great pain. There were times when I finished an Epic in genuine tears, and not because the protagonist I embodied in the memory had been sobbing.

For once, my Mindbank offered me little comfort.

Before long, I found myself sharing my woes with my mother again. To my dismay, I did not manage to finish my story before she began to snicker, adding salt to my wounds.

"Foolish girl! If your husband really wanted to hide an affair, why would he give you access to his Mindbank? Did he not hand you his Scroller?"

I frowned. "I'm not sure I understand."

"Wouldn't seeing his history give you some peace of mind?"

"That would be an invasion of privacy, Ma. Have you heard of the punishments for trespassing? The penalties can be severe."

"Silly girl. Maybe that's the case for strangers, but do you think the Party courts have time to hear such cases from a married couple? Unless a family of renown decides to pursue a divorce, when has there been any real consequences for a little snooping?" She scoffed. "Have you forgotten that he's your husband? I thought modern couples shared everything these days."

Ma's face softened. "Perhaps Ming left his Scroller behind on purpose. Maybe he meant to give you permission. Either way, he will never know, so long as you don't let slip what you witness in his memories."

My stomach began to churn for the first time since we replaced the proteins in our diet with Nutrilent. What would the perfect Qin wife do?

I opened my mouth to ask. But before I could, Ma disconnected from my Mindbank, and I found myself alone again.

IF I WERE THE PERFECT WIFE, I MIGHT HAVE BEEN ABLE TO RESIST. But I was never considered an ideal woman by any standard. I soon convinced myself that it would be in my husband's best interests too, if I could relieve my insecurities with a peek inside his memories. Perhaps Ma was right, and my husband had given me his implicit permission by leaving behind the backup device to his memories.

I tried to relax. I opened a new carton of Nutrilent, optimized for my digestive system, and emptied the sweetened puree into my mouth. When I didn't feel any better, I lay on my bed and took a few deep breaths. Then, picking up my husband's Scroller, I established the connection between our Mindbanks. To my relief, a cursory scan of his device revealed that his memories were neatly arranged by themes: Arctic, Friendship, Exercise . . . Grateful that I did not need to use the internal search engine, I selected one of the memories stored under the subtheme of Running. I tried my best to stay calm as the sensations from his purchased and lived histories soon replaced the nervous tension in my stomach.

How strange it can feel to assume another person's form! As my consciousness flowed into the mind of the memory's protagonist, I came to accept that I was now an adolescent boy named Ming—so it was one of my husband's own experiences. Savoring the sensations of his youthful body, his muscles taut in a crouching position, I became aware that we were waiting for a gunshot to signal the start of some competition. Before my mind could register the bang, I felt a burst of speed from my legs, then the wind on my back as my new body surged over the hurdles to the ribboned finish line . . .

I had not known that Ming was a runner. What else had he not told me? I suddenly recalled the strange objects I once discovered in my husband's desk: a delicate pink gold watch that no longer ticked, a dozen wooden panels spreading out into a fan painting of an Elder riding a red-crowned bird, hoodies branded with logos from former American-white tech companies, and most strikingly, an enormous loincloth for which I could not fathom any explanation.

Had he confiscated the items through his official duties as a senior Censor? If so, why had he not disposed of them? Out of respect, I had closed the drawer and pretended to have seen nothing, but should I have confronted him? Before I could chase the thought, I found my consciousness overwhelmed by a sense of incredible freedom in my chest. For what must have been a quarter hour, I reveled in the crowd's thunderous cheers as I circled the track with a medal around my neck, glinting under the stadium lights.

How odd our people had once been, racing each other in the polluted air. Still, I took deep pleasure in the cool breeze as it brushed blissfully against my skin. For a split second, I even considered trusting my husband. Because Ming manually severed the connection to his Mindbank every night, none of his recent runs were recorded. What was the point, then, of looking through his old memories? Now that I knew he had a history of running in his youth, I had nothing to gain from violating his trust.

But since I was already trespassing, would it hurt to explore a few more memories? And so I picked the theme so intriguingly labeled "Friendship," wanting to see who else had played an important role in my husband's life. Despite our forty moons of marriage, I had met only a handful of his friends via Mindbank. The fact that he so rarely spoke about anyone beside his fellow Censors made me curious why that theme contained so many memories.

Instantly, I found myself in the mind of a Qin male who was not Ming. Only this time instead of preparing for a race, my new body was violently thrusting into the nether regions of some American-white woman!

We moaned her name in unison.

"Fantasia! Fantasia!" Our heart pounded like birds frantically smashing their wings against a cage. His intense pleasure flowed through my veins, even as a deep anger began to course through my physical body.

She had the palest skin I had ever laid eyes on.

My hands were trembling. In the stranger's memory, I stared

deeply into Fantasia's eyes. She had curly red hair, hazel irises, and lips of dusky pink. She was beautiful.

I gasped, then logged out. But moments later, I returned to his Mindbank and found myself in the form of another stranger, receiving a sensual massage. Once again, the object of desire was a woman of American-white descent.

I shivered. The entire theme consisted of sexual memories featuring pale-skinned women. What if every night since he began to "run," Ming had instead been visiting those notorious hotels filled with Fourth World migrants known to fulfill the fantasies of unsavory Qin men?

Hot and cold waves of anger and dread alternated through my body. Part of me wanted to believe that this was only a misunderstanding. But no, it made sense—why else had he refused my efforts at procreation? I struggled to accept this new reality. How could my husband punish me this way? How could he harbor such twisted desires for women who had never studied the history of our great Party? Why would he favor them over me—I who had worked so hard to fulfill the duties of a Qin wife over the past forty moons? It was wrong for him to desire women of other skin, even if there was no law against it. Especially women of a race that had once subjugated our people, even if we were the ones in control now.

What if his power over those women was precisely the appeal?

I stood from our bed and went to the living room window. How much coin had he paid for those fantasies? A sound escaped my mouth; only afterward did I recognize it as a sob.

Shame coursed beneath my skin. I wiped my cheeks. I stared down through the tinted solar windows, wondering whether it might be raining beneath those clouds.

"DAUGHTER."

I listened intently for Ma's advice. More than a moon had passed since my first foray into my husband's Mindbank, and I could no longer keep my guilt to myself.

"Daughter, listen. You should count yourself lucky," Ma said. "It could be much worse, yes?"

She did not wait for me to respond. "At least we know that Ming is unlikely to leave your marriage. His parents would never consent to any union with an American-white woman . . ."

I no longer heard Ma's voice over my thumping heart.

What did she know? Over the past moon, had she doubled her daily intake of Nutrilent so that her body might more closely re-semble the hourglass figures of Ming's fantasies? In the evenings, had she suffered through every memory, replaying Fantasia's moans for self-enlightenment? Had she considered dyeing her hair red? All the while feeling conflicted about whether she should even try to save her marriage? After all, I had discovered other Epics in his Mindbank too, banned content that would place both our families in danger if they came to light.

How could Ma begin to understand, when I could not reveal any knowledge of those illicit memories to her? The tragic love story of a Qin-born activist before the War. A forbidden relation-ship between an Ambassador-Regent's son and an American-white orphan. Memory Epics that referenced the Incineration of Ri-Ben or boldly recited the poems of a Desert Colonist. Why would Ming risk everything for these stories? If we were convicted for harboring such treasonous content, all our memory assets might be taken from us, confiscated for the Criminal Archives. They could disappear us from history altogether; the Party had the power to mandate that any memories containing traces of our family's existence be purged from the public domain. For the first time, I understood why Ming had hidden his seemingly innocuous collection of peculiarities in that secret drawer, given how significant a role some of the items had played in his most seditious Memory Epics.

And yet, my husband's greatest betrayal remained Fantasia.

While there were more dangerous memories in his possession, it was his desire for this American-white woman which I struggled to accept most. What choice did I have though, except to stay? Stay and dutifully protect his secrets, so that our families could continue their shared fantasy of having raised two honorable Qin citizens, in a stable marriage and living in a respectable Tower . . .

"Daughter, if it would help, I am willing to transfer you some intimate memories too—"

"Ma, no!" The silence lingered. "No, please.

"Everything is okay," I lied. Then, for the first time, I was the one to terminate our Mindbank link.

THE NIGHT I PLANNED TO CONFESS TO MING ABOUT ENTERING HIS Mindbank, I stared out our magnificent windows, contemplating whether his inevitable anger at my betrayal would result in the end of our marriage. I awaited his return from beneath the clouds.

Uncertainties still plagued me. What if my husband had been telling the truth? What if he had truly been running, preferring the rush of endorphins to the synthetic chemicals in Nutrilent? Maybe he had never cheated on me in the flesh. Did other Qin husbands also purchase memories featuring women like Fantasia? Was it so awful that he needed to address his sexual desires this way, if it meant that he could meet the more important responsibilities of our marriage? Didn't we all store one or two memories in our Mind-bank that might be more prudent to erase? Had he otherwise not been a good husband, sharing secrets gleaned from his honorable role, like how the Party had cleaned the skies?

Lately, I've been replaying certain memories from my childhood.

I remembered frolicking outside as a young girl, naively breathing in the smog. Many times, I refused to return to our Tower after the sky turned dark, because I wanted to keep admiring the moon's glow without any interference from the solar glass. It made me wonder—when exactly had the air become so polluted to justify the Party's command for us to permanently ascend? And how did they decide which permits for the Outside to approve?

My mother's face flashed in my mind, her forehead creased in consternation. In all her lectures, had she once cast doubt on the Party? Had she ever questioned if what our society valued in a Qin wife was what all women should strive for? Had she once taken my side in an argument with my husband during my marriage? Even after she learned of the vile memories Ming held in his Mindbank, she still encouraged me to stay with him, no matter how much distress his secrets had caused me.

Nauseous, I felt a wave of acid climb my throat. Without thinking, I swallowed. My esophagus burned.

I fell to my knees and waited for my panic to subside. When it resolved, I leaned my shoulder against the window, smudging the glass as I tried to stand.

I was disgusted. By the vomit, by my mother's cowardice, but most of all, by myself. Wiping my mouth with a sleeve, I suddenly felt an urge to escape, not wanting to stay in this Tower for another second. I wrapped a black shawl around my face, as if the extra layer could defend my lungs from the toxins, and stumbled out of my apartment toward the Accelerator. Already I found myself dreading the heat of the Outside. I closed my eyes and tried to recall the feeling of uneven pavement. Mindbanks were the mechanism by which we experienced the world now—why did I need to risk my body? Worse, what if I were stopped by some Party officer in the lobby and asked to show my Outside permit? Certainly, I could lie and claim that I had simply descended out of worry for my husband—but what if they didn't believe me?

Still, I persisted.

The Accelerator carried me to the ground. I barely felt the drop in my stomach before the ride was over. Exiting its doors and walking toward the entrance, I was stunned to see that the lobby was empty save for a dozen humming metal air filters overhead. I realized then that the mere anxiety of being caught Outside was enough to keep good citizens such as myself in the Tower. A wave of incredulity passed through me; I was not even aware of the exact punishment for such an offense! Yet the Party had so effortlessly used my fear against me. For a second, I felt a pit of anger in my stomach. Then, as I began moving again, it transformed into a sense of excitement, even rejuvenation. Waving goodbye to the old AI monitors watching over our lobby, I felt oddly self-conscious, as if those cameras were arching their sensors due to confusion.

An old memory of heat and humidity surfaced in my Mindbank: the day of my wedding, when I moved from my family home into this Tower. I recalled Ma helping me change into five different qipaos throughout the day and the joy on Ming's face every time he saw me in another dress. I remembered the suffocation in my chest, the beads of sweat stuck to my back and the heavy weight I had carried in my heart, the fear that I might never fulfill the lofty duties of a Qin wife. Had I ever been able to expel that stone from my stomach? I had survived that wedding day. I would survive tonight as well.

As I approached the front entrance of the Tower, I was reminded of the nightmare in which I watched my lungs darken from within. As the mysterious rot spread across my arms and legs, my limbs became frozen in space until my body crumbled into a pile of ash; then a single yellow chrysanthemum sprouted from the fresh earth.

Shaking my head, I gradually brought myself out of the memory. The final barrier to the Outside was a mere door; I pushed it. When it swung back faster than I could react, the glass gently collided with my forehead. Then a cool breeze swept against my face.

The Outside. It was right there.

Still, I could not move. I held my breath, feeling the pressure building in my chest. How could I be certain that the air was not poisonous? Yet if I did not take the risk, how would I ever know? As my mother's face came to mind once more, I pushed the glass again. Only this time, before the door could swing back, I took three steps forward and crossed into the open.

For the first time since my marriage, I had abandoned the Tower. Relinquishing the last of my fears, I took a breath. Would my lungs turn black, as they had in my nightmare? If death came for me now, I took comfort that at least it would be from a choice I made myself.

Beneath the gentle moonlight illuminating the white walls of the Tower, I blinked. The moon was no longer obfuscated by smog, its light no longer dimmed by solar glass. My strength returned with each new breath.

To my wonder, the skies had been cleaned. Just as Ming said.

Oh, thank you, glorious Party! I relished the silent beauty of the evening, removing the shawl from my face and letting it fall to the earth. And that is when I saw him.

My husband. Racing in my direction. Returning home.

His wet shirt glowed in the moonlight. His legs were pumping, but his face glowed with contentment. Sweat ran down his scarred face. When he saw me, the corners of his mouth blossomed into a smile as wide as any I had witnessed in our marriage.

Delighted, he pointed a finger toward a majestic banyan I had never seen before, its thick roots wrapped around our building. Its branches ran up the walls, wild and rampant. Nobody had predetermined the banyan's growth. Yet from above, I had not even known of its existence.

The tree curled its limbs around the Tower, embracing my home with a warmth I had never felt while living there. But when I raised my palm warily to greet my husband, a gust of wind nearly blew me over. Flailing my arms, I saw from the corner of my vision that he was laughing. Laughing at his own wife's misfortune! I felt the flush on my cheeks disappear. And as the gale tore at my skin, while I stubbornly tried to stand in place, I realized that if I were to ask for my husband's forgiveness for my trespasses—if I accepted his sexual perversions and remained in the relationship—I would also be surrendering the last of my power.

It wasn't fair. Didn't I also deserve the right to decide what was important in my marriage? Regardless of how the Party dictated a woman in my position should act, I deserved that agency. So when the wind started to die down, I silently vowed that I would no longer allow myself to be bound by the shackles of society—not to him, nor anyone else in our world.

All at once, I no longer feared or envied any woman.

Not even Fantasia.

I wanted this newfound freedom to last forever. In that moment, I resolved to keep all the memories I had accessed over the past moon, knowing that my husband would never pursue my theft and risk an investigation into his Mindbank.

When he stopped laughing, I started to sprint toward him, almost tripping over myself. His footsteps shuddered to a halt. Waving his arms above his head, Ming called for me to slow; I pretended it was only the wind howling. As confusion spread across his features, I saw that, apart from his scars, his face was no more exceptional than mine. In the soft glow of the moon, I reveled for an instant in how beautiful I must appear to him, the luster of my skin more angelic than any American-white woman animated by his Mindbank.

Above us, the clouds shifted and occluded the moon. Beneath the shadows, his scars were nearly invisible. Then his face began to disappear, becoming as forgettable as a distant memory, as banal as any fantasy of marriage conjured from Qin's past.

Before the man could cry out again, I raced past him toward the bliss of the night.

FINAL MESSAGE

████████ at ██ : ██████

My mother adored the wind.

Not only when we felt a warm breeze against our bodies, but also when a squall ripped at our faces or pushed us backward during one of our walks. My mother would joyously spread her freckled arms to greet the wind, and I would wonder why she reacted this way to such ordinary weather.

When I asked, she told me that I wouldn't understand.

One day, I'll share my memories with you, she said. *I'll let them explain everything.*

Even when her knees began to ache, my mother never missed our weekly strolls. There were many opportunities for her to tell me her stories, but she was always more interested in hearing about what struggles I was facing in my life. In her frailest moments, the only change I noticed was how tightly she held my hand during our walks, as if some unseen force might blow her away if my fingers accidentally let go.

Why did she not trust me with all her memories when she was alive? She could have told me about her first marriage in the Towers, how she wrested back control of her life long ago. In conversation, she had only ever alluded to her past in the vaguest terms, especially the hundred moons when the Party confined all citizens to the Towers, before the sky became clean again. Even after going through her Mindbank, there was so much more that I wanted to know.

We could have decided what to do with her memories together.

As a family.

Had she merely been afraid of my questions? Why was she so avoidant, cowardly even? Perhaps my mother was an ordinary woman after all—and I am just a son who loved her.

DID YOU EMBRACE YOUR FREEDOM? WHEN YOU RELIVED MY mother's memories, did you experience them in a different order? Or did you accept the status quo, the sequence I determined in your stead?

Forgive me. I have no right to reproach you if you did not rebel against the order. Most of us were not born to be revolutionaries; you already know that I am no hero. Unless you were Reincarnated from the generation before the armless swimmer, the Party has been in power far longer than you or I have existed. Is it so strange if we no longer remember how to resist? Especially as they expand their control to include everything we are allowed to recall?

Still, I hope you can find the courage to tell your own truth. Even if your resistance begins as small as a bedtime story to your child; there is no need to risk everything you hold dear. The Censors will soon discover this trove of memories. So be quick: denounce me as a traitor before the Red Guards can find you and threaten your family.

Trust that I will not blame you. I acknowledge that resistance can be a privilege. Even in these memories, whether the stories revolved around immigrants before Qin, forbidden lovers, or the Chrysanthemum Virus, many of our protagonists made difficult choices to save their families. Or themselves. But if I have learned anything from my mother's secrets, it is that resistance can also be necessary for survival. Many times, it was the least powerful in the Memory Epics who pushed back against the dominant forces. Even if their small acts did not succeed in overthrowing the systems and people in control, they still found ways to fight.

For so long, my mother shielded me from these truths. But in the end, I believe she accepted that we both had a greater responsibility to these stories than to ourselves. She could have asked for her Mindbank to be deleted when she died; but in her final decision to pass down these dangerous memories, she must have recognized a strength in me that I'd never appreciated in myself. Out of everything I inherited, perhaps that was her greatest gift.

I miss her dearly. In my eyes, she remains my first hero.

Should you choose to denounce me, I will understand your decision. All I ask in return is that you remember this as well—that you are not alone. Whether you are suffering or feeling powerless, you stand with countless others throughout history who faced oppression and fought to hold on to the love and beauty in their lives. You are not alone; if you recall nothing else from these memories, please hold on to this feeling of solidarity, this unyielding wind carrying our dreams of a better future.

Nobody can take that away.

It belongs to us all. I promise you: it will always belong to us all.

ACKNOWLEDGMENTS

■ My Wife ■ My Parents ■ Teachers: Dean Bakopoulos, Lesley Arimah, Jamel Brinkley, Marisa Silver, Reese Kwon, Vanessa Hua, Ibi Kaslik, Pasha Malla, Amy Hempel, Michael Knight, Christine Schutt, Ted Thompson, Debra Allbery ■ LARDY: Daniel Tam Claiborne, Lillian Huang Cummins, Annette Wong, Roseanne Pereira ■ WW: Terri Leker, Juli Min, Sarah Audsley, Kate Campbell, Artis Henderson, Courtney Han, Neck Cobras ■ Writing mentors & friends: Jason Mott, Vincent Lam, Lauren Groff, Lillian Li, Omar El-Akkad, Tessa Hulls, Sequoia Nagamatsu, Erika Swyler, Clare Beams, George Saunders, Crystal Hana Kim, Tony Doerr, Simon Han, Dominic Smith, Nina McConigley, Mike Zapata, Kathy Wang, Ai Jiang ■ Denne Michele Norris, Karissa Chen, our fierce debut Slack ■ Ryan Chapman, Amanda Fatemi, Ariel Goldenthal ■ Kaveh Akbar for his poems ■ Millay Colony, VSC, Sewanee, Tin House, FLR, 4th Estate ■ Mao Mao, Grandparents, Da Ma ■ First readers: Emily Chau, Sithara Kodali, Yen Tan, Diana Wu David, Neal Bennett, Elise Liu, Leo Ding, Teddy Kuhn, Rocio Rebollo, Yue Li, Amac ■ Wedding bros: Jacob Younan, Trey Teo, Tommy Yuin, Punit Shah, Jeff Sun, Darío De Filippis, Kevin Yuen ■ From my other life: Katelyn Donnelly, Amar Kumar, Scott Moyers, Robert Wheaton, Ryan Davies, Brett, Tim, Avrum ■ Trellis & team: Allison Malecha, Elizabeth Pratt, Niki Chang, Sean Daily, Kathy Daneman ■ Mariner team: Ellie Anderson, Deanna Bailey, Dale Rohrbaugh, Jennifer Chung, Eliza Rosenberry, Tavia Kowalchuk ■ Cover: Ploy Siripant ■ M&S team: Stephanie Sinclair, Chalista Andadari, Tonia Addison, Sarah Howland, Kimberlee Kemp ■
■ Anita Chong, Jessica Vestuto, Michelle Brower, Natalie Edwards ■